All Along

D. E. Haggerty

Copyright © 2025 D.E. Haggerty

All rights reserved.

D.E. Haggerty asserts the moral right to be identified as the author of this work.

ISBN: 9789083465531

All Along is a work of fiction. The names, characters, places, and incidents portrayed in it are the product of the author's imagination. Any resemblance to actual persons, living or dead, events or locations is entirely coincidental.

All rights reserved. No part of this publication may be reproduced, stored in a retrieval system, or transmitted, in any form or by any means, electronic, mechanical, photocopying, recording or otherwise, without the prior permission of the author.

No portion of this book may be reproduced in any form without written permission from the publisher or author, except as permitted by U.S. copyright law.

Also by D.E. Haggerty

Before It Was Love
After The Vows
While We Waited
How to Date a Rockstar
How to Love a Rockstar
How to Fall For a Rockstar
How to Be a Rockstar's Girlfriend
How to Catch a Rockstar
My Forever Love
Forever For You
Just For Forever
Stay For Forever
Only Forever
Meet Disaster
Meet Not
Meet Dare
Meet Hate
Bragg's Truth
Bragg's Love
Perfect Bragg

Bragg's Match
Bragg's Christmas
A Hero for Hailey
A Protector for Phoebe
A Soldier for Suzie
A Fox for Faith
A Christmas for Chrissie
A Valentine for Valerie
A Love for Lexi
About Face
At Arm's Length
Hands Off
Knee Deep
Molly's Misadventures

Also by D.E. Haggerty

Before It Was Love
After The Vows
While We Waited
How to Date a Rockstar
How to Love a Rockstar
How to Fall For a Rockstar
How to Be a Rockstar's Girlfriend
How to Catch a Rockstar
My Forever Love
Forever For You
Just For Forever
Stay For Forever
Only Forever
Meet Disaster
Meet Not
Meet Dare
Meet Hate
Bragg's Truth
Bragg's Love
Perfect Bragg

Bragg's Match
Bragg's Christmas
A Hero for Hailey
A Protector for Phoebe
A Soldier for Suzie
A Fox for Faith
A Christmas for Chrissie
A Valentine for Valerie
A Love for Lexi
About Face
At Arm's Length
Hands Off
Knee Deep
Molly's Misadventures

Chapter 1

Maya – a shy woman who refuses to be pushed around by her best friends. Mostly.

MAYA

"I'm not doing it."

I wish I could say I shouted those words or maybe stomped my foot to make my point, but I'm barely speaking above a whisper. Being shy sucks sometimes.

"Come on." My friend, Chloe, elbows me. "It'll be a blast."

I hold my ground. "I'm not writing a love message in a bottle."

Why did I let my friends drag me out to the *Hearts Beneath the Waves Festival*? I should have known one of them – either Chloe, Sophia, Nova, or Paisley – would pull some kind of stunt.

During Valentine's Day weekend, our hometown of Smuggler's Rest along with the rest of the island of Smuggler's Hideaway transforms into an underwater dreamscape. There are romantic mermaid statues, sea creatures holding hearts, and smuggling barrels turned into flower vases.

But it's not a Smuggler's Hideaway festival without quirky activities. The *Hearts Beneath the Waves Festival* includes a love parade, siren's serenade singing contest, sweetheart race, and mermaid's blessing ceremony. To top it all off, there's a seafoam ball tonight. Which I will not be attending even if I have to pretend I got buried under all the romance books in my house.

"It'll be fun," Sophia claims.

I fail to understand what is 'fun' about writing an anonymous love note in a bottle for any festival-goer to read. Or act on? I shiver. I don't want a date with some random tourist.

"Why would she write an anonymous love letter when the man she wants can't read the letter?" Paisley asks.

Nova slaps her shoulder. "Leave Maya alone."

Paisley blinks in confusion. It's not an act. My big-brained friend doesn't understand what the problem is.

She pushes her glasses up her nose. "I don't understand. I'm defending Maya."

Nova scowls at her. "You brought up Caleb. After we agreed not to bring him up anymore."

"I didn't say his name. You did."

They begin to squabble and I tune them out. *Caleb.* The boy who helped me climb down the monkey bars when I was in second grade is now a soldier fighting our country's enemies somewhere overseas. He's also my pen pal. And the man I imagine every hero in every romance novel I read resembles.

But it's not to be. Caleb isn't for me. We're friends. Nothing more. Nothing less. No matter how much I may wish otherwise.

"What if Caleb finds out she wrote someone else a love letter and gets all jealous and rushes back to Smuggler's Hideaway to make it clear to all smugglers and mermaids alike that Maya belongs to him?" Sophia asks.

I bite my lip as I imagine Caleb arriving back on the island to stake his claim on me. My stomach warms and I nearly swoon. I'd star in my very own romance novel! He'd shove my suitor out of his way before claiming me with a searing kiss.

"If Maya isn't going to write a love message, I will." Chloe marches to the message in the bottle station. We hurry after her.

Sophia swipes the pen from her. "You can't write an anonymous love message in a bottle. You're married."

Chloe waggles her eyebrows. "Imagine how mad my dear husband will be when he finds out."

"I don't understand." Paisley purses her lips. "Do you want Lucas to be mad at you?"

Sophia giggles. "Oh, she wants Lucas to be mad at her all right."

Because apparently, Lucas punishes Chloe in sexy ways. I don't know exactly how, but their relationship reminds me of one of those BDSM books that were so popular a few years back. Those books? Phew. They made me all hot and bothered.

Nova moans and grabs her stomach. I rush to her. My pregnant friend is nearing her due date and probably shouldn't be on her feet all day.

"Are you okay? Is Sprog okay? Do you need to sit down?"

I don't wait for her to answer before leading her to a table set out on the sidewalk in front of *Smuggler's Cove*. The restaurant has placed a bunch of tables outside for people to watch the love parade.

"Stop fussing over me," Nova says once she sits down. "Hudson fusses over me enough."

Chloe plops down on a chair next to her. "Because he's your baby daddy."

"He's, my partner. Baby daddy sounds like we had a one-night stand."

I giggle. "Didn't you get pregnant with Sprog after a one-night stand?"

Nova has been obsessed with Hudson since over a decade ago when he was on the football team in high school. She even tried out to be a cheerleader to impress him. She didn't impress anyone during her try-out considering several cheerleaders ended up at the hospital. There was only one broken bone, though.

Sophia checks her watch. "We should probably head on over to the brewery and make sure things are running smoothly."

The brewery is our brewery – *Five Fathoms Brewing*. We founded the brewery after we returned to the island after college and we now operate it together.

Chloe is the hospitality manager since she couldn't sit behind a desk for eight hours if someone chained her to the chair. Sophia is the marketing manager. She used to work for some fancy schmancy marketing firm in Atlanta before coming home last year and promptly falling in love with her brother's best friend.

Nova is the sales manager. She smiles at prospective clients and they fall at her feet. Paisley is the actual brewer. My nerdy friend is obsessed with trying out new flavors. Lucky for the brewery, her ideas are genius. Except for the time she decided to test the limits of how hoppy an IPA could get. Not her best idea.

And, finally, there's me. I'm the financial manager for the brewery. What can I say? I love numbers as much as Paisley loves facts.

I stand. "I'll go. You're meeting Flynn here in a few minutes."

Sophia sighs and the love she has for her fiancé is plain to see. I love it. I love how all of my friends are heroines in their very own romance novels.

Paisley joins me. "I'll go with you."

Paisley is the only other single person left in our group of friends.

"Can you check in on Addy?" Chloe asks as she waves goodbye to us. "It's her first time being in charge for the day."

I nod to Chloe before walking toward the brewery with Paisley. *Five Fathoms Brewing* is located in an old barn a few blocks from downtown. It's not a long walk. Although, to be fair, nothing is far in Smuggler's Rest.

The island isn't very big either. There are three towns on the island – Smuggler's Rest, Pirate's Perch, and Rogue Landing –

but all of the fun festivals happen in Smuggler's Rest. It's also where my friends and I grew up.

"Are you all right?" Paisley asks once we're away from the crowds.

"All right? Why wouldn't I be all right?"

"You always get sad when we mention Caleb."

"I'm not sad," I deny.

"I disagree. Your chin trembles and your eyes get dull whenever his name is spoken out loud."

Leave it to my fact obsessed friend to come up with evidence.

I sigh. "I'm fine. Caleb is my friend."

"But you want more."

I shake my head. "It doesn't matter what I want."

"Why not? Your needs and wants are valid. Why shouldn't you get everything you want?"

She doesn't get it. I can want Caleb all I want. It doesn't change a thing. We're friends.

"Caleb is half a world away," I remind her.

"He can't remain a soldier forever."

He's managed to remain a soldier for twelve years, which feels pretty darn close to forever.

I shrug. "He might not come home when he gets out of the Army."

I'd be surprised if he did. He doesn't return home for any of the holidays. And I know he gets thirty days of leave each year. He could easily come back to the island for at least a week a year. But he doesn't. He hasn't stepped foot on Smuggler's Hideaway in over a decade.

Sometimes I get the feeling he's avoiding me, which is silly. We're merely friends. He doesn't make decisions based on little old me.

We reach the brewery. The bar, restaurant, and our offices are in a barn we restored. The actual brewing happens in a warehouse on the opposite side of the parking lot.

"I need to check on the beer," Paisley says and makes a beeline for the warehouse.

My phone beeps in my pocket. I pull it out and frown when I notice it's a message from the postal service. A package I sent to Caleb has been returned with a 'sender unknown' stamp. What in the world? I used the same address as I always do.

Is something wrong? Did Caleb move without telling me? Is it even called moving when you're in the military? Despite being pen pals for a decade, I still don't understand all the Army lingo.

I pace the parking lot as I consider what to do. Caleb doesn't like it when I phone without prior notice but I have no choice. I need to phone him. I need to know if he's okay.

I dial his number but the call doesn't connect. Strange. I try again. This time it rings. Phew.

"The number you have dialed is not in service, please check the number and dial again, or ask the operator for assistance."

I gasp. Not in service? How can Caleb's number not be in service? It's the same number he's used for a decade.

I shove down the panic. There's nothing to panic about. If Caleb was hurt or injured, the smuggler grapevine would have let me know by now.

He's probably fine. He's probably on some super secret mission he couldn't tell me about.

Yep. That must be it.

Chapter 2

Caleb – a soldier who doesn't know who he is if he isn't a soldier anymore

CALEB

I scowl at the 'Welcome to Smuggler's Hideaway' sign as I drive onto the island. Welcome, my ass. I'm not here because I want to be.

I don't have a choice. I need time to heal. Time to lick my wounds away from prying eyes and questions I can't – won't – answer. Which is why I'm keeping to myself until I'm better.

Once I'm healed, things will be different.

In the meantime, knowing Maya is here on the island – nearly within touching distance – will be torture. I have some experience with torture. But this won't be similar to being in the sandbox. Those occurrences never touched my heart. Not the way Maya does.

I drive through Smuggler's Rest but I don't pay attention to the town or people or whatever crazy festival is going on now. There's always some crazy festival happening on the island. Smugglers love to party.

I keep my eyes focused on the road and pray no one notices me. Although, I doubt anyone would recognize me anyway. It's been twelve years since I stepped foot on the island. I've stayed away for one reason and one reason only – Maya.

Everything comes back to her.

When the town fades behind me, I blow out the breath I didn't realize I was holding. No one saw me. No one's chasing after me. A twinge of regret pokes at me, but I ignore it. Maya doesn't want to be around me now anyway.

I glance down at my legs. My legs are covered by a pair of jeans but in my mind, I see blood, gore, and bone sticking out of a gaping wound. I force those thoughts away. It's the past.

I adjust my leg and pain shoots up my foot to my groin. I grit my teeth. Not as much in the past as it needs to be.

I follow the road from Smuggler's Rest toward Rogue's Landing. *Hideaway Haven Resort* should be halfway between the towns.

The resort didn't exist when I lived here. Hudson Clark, who was two years ahead of me in high school, built the resort when he came back to the island after his career in the NFL crashed.

He also owns the cabin I rented. It should be near the border to his resort. I follow the GPS directions past the resort and turn left onto an unpaved road.

It's a good thing I rented a truck for the time I'll be back on the island since the road is uneven and bumpy. Every time the truck hits a bump, I grit my teeth as pain shoots up my leg. It's a relief when a cabin comes into view.

It's small and isn't much but I don't need much. All I need is a bed to sleep in and room to do my exercises.

I park in front of the cabin and slide out of the truck. My knee buckles when my leg takes my weight – I've been sitting too long, but I wanted to make it to the island before dark. I use my hold on the truck to keep my balance. I will not be collapsing again. Never again.

"Caleb?" someone shouts.

I squint and notice a man standing on the porch.

"I'm Caleb."

The man jogs down the steps toward me. I recognize him. It's Hudson. He's moving well for someone whose ankle was blown out by an illegal tackle during a football game.

Hope and determination fill me. If he can do it, so can I.

"Sorry, man," Hudson says when he reaches me. "I didn't recognize you."

I run a hand over my jaw. I barely recognize myself without a bushy beard but I shaved it off the second I was stateside. I don't need a reminder of why I'm not overseas staring at me every morning in the mirror.

I grunt and he chuckles. "And I'm supposed to be the grumpy one."

My brow wrinkles. "Don't seem grumpy to me."

"I'm not as grumpy as I used to be. Love will do that to a man."

I'm confused. Maya's letters never mentioned any news about Hudson being in love. Considering my pen pal is obsessed with love and romance, she would have told me if the famous former NFL player had fallen in love.

Although, I haven't received a letter from her in some time. Correction. I threw away her letters in a fit of rage before reading them. Regret knocks on my consciousness but I ignore it. If I let my regrets in, they'll overwhelm me.

I clear my throat. "Love?"

"You know Nova Myers?"

I nod. Of course, I know Nova. She's one of Maya's best friends. Together they founded a brewery with the rest of their friends. I'm not surprised *Five Fathoms Brewing* is a success. Those five women can do anything they put their minds to. The island is lucky they didn't decide to start a criminal empire.

"She's my woman and she's having my baby."

My eyes widen in surprise. Of all the things I expected him to say, announcing Nova's having his baby didn't even make the list.

Jealousy whirls around in my stomach. I want to be the one announcing the woman I love is having my baby. But I'm not. And I won't be anytime soon. Maybe never again. Not after—

Nope. I shove those thoughts away. My guilt belongs in the box with my regrets.

"Congrats."

"Thanks." He motions to the cabin. "Can I help you with your stuff?"

I reach inside the truck and grab my duffle. "I'm good."

Hudson nods and leads me to the cabin. He unlocks the door and pushes it open before handing me the key.

"It isn't much, but it's clean and isolated."

Isolated is exactly what I need. I glance around the interior. The area is split into two. On the left are the living room and kitchen. On the right are two doors. One should lead to the bedroom and the other to the bathroom.

"It'll do," I say and step inside.

"I'll leave you to it."

I reach to shut the door but he stops and whirls around. "By the way, I'm having a party on Saturday."

"Not much for parties."

"I figured you'd say as much, but you're welcome none the less."

I grunt my thanks before closing the door to shut him and the world out.

Chapter 3

"If my life is a romance novel, I know who I want to play the hero." ~ *Maya*

MAYA

I frown when I notice how crowded Nova and Hudson's chalet is. Paisley pats my shoulder.

"Don't be afraid. Pretend this is one of your romance novels."

If she only knew. I'm constantly pretending my life is a romance novel. It's how I manage to enter rooms with large groups of people.

"Thanks."

"Always. I'm always here for you."

She is. I have a great group of friends. But Sophia and Chloe aren't around as much anymore since they've found love. And now Nova is all loved up, too.

Soon I'll be all alone again since Paisley will probably fall in love before me. It's kind of hard to fall in love when you've been obsessed with a boy you went to high school with for most of your life.

A boy who's now a man in the military and is always stationed overseas. Mostly in really scary places he won't tell me about. A man who is merely my pen pal buddy. And will never be more.

Paisley herds me toward the bar. "Let's get a drink."

I drag my feet. "I'm driving."

"This is Nova's baby shower. I'm certain she has non-alcoholic drinks."

Drat. There goes my excuse for staying on the edge of the crowd.

Pretend this is a romance novel. I imagine I'm the youngest daughter of a duke being forced to attend a ball against her will. Her father is ready for her to marry, but she's in love with the gardener. He's forbidden since he's a commoner.

By the time Paisley shoves a non-alcoholic beer in my hand, I'm warming up to my story. I bet the gardener is sexy. I imagine he's over six feet tall and has bulging muscles. I add blond hair and blue eyes to the image. Maybe a cute dimple to soften his face.

Paisley hands me a pink ribbon and brings me out of my fantasy. "What's this?"

"Nova and Hudson are doing a gender reveal. Guests are supposed to pick a pink or blue ribbon based on what gender they think the baby is." She waves her blue ribbon. "There were only two left."

"The baby is going to be a girl. I know it."

"Which is why I gave you the pink ribbon. Come on. The reveal is happening outside."

I hurry to follow Paisley out the back doors. There are just as many people outside but it doesn't feel as scary when there are no walls barreling down on me.

Paisley leads me to where Chloe and Sophia are standing. I scan the area for Chloe's stepdaughter. "Where's Natalia?"

Chloe points to the pool. "She's over there."

"When did Nova get a pool?" Paisley asks.

"Hudson had it built for her as a present for her baby shower," Sophia says. "You know how she hates to swim in the ocean."

Chloe giggles. "I accept full credit. Nova has some kick on her. She nearly broke my nose."

"You shouldn't have scared her by tugging on her leg," I say.

Paisley's nose wrinkles. "Why she was convinced a shark was trying to drown her is a mystery to me. Sharks don't have hands."

"She panicked. No one thinks rationally when they panic."

"Which explains why you ran out of biology class shouting 'the English are coming' when you were supposed to give your presentation," Sophia says.

"I don't understand why we had to give a presentation anyway. It was biology class," I mutter.

"Public speaking is a valuable skill," Paisley says.

I snort. "You fall asleep whenever I talk about the quarterly numbers."

"Numbers are boring," Chloe declares.

Not to me they aren't. They're reliable and dependable. And, best of all, numbers mean I don't need to speak to anyone when it comes to my job as the financial manager for *Five Fathoms Brewing*. Except for those pesky clients who refuse to pay. Lucky for me, an email will often suffice.

Numbers aren't as exciting as romance, though. If I could write romance books, I'd be a writer and spend my days dreaming up ways for the hero and heroine to fall in love. But one creative writing class in college taught me I have no writing skills whatsoever. So, numbers it is.

Chloe claps her hands. "It's time for the gender reveal. I'm totally popping the balloon with the color."

She forces her way through the crowd until she's in the front. "Me first."

She throws her dart at the board filled with balloons. Water splashes out of the balloon she hit but there's no color. She scowls. "I want to go again."

Sophia shoves her out of the way. "My turn."

Chloe stomps back to us. "No fair. I'm sure I would have gotten it right with my second balloon."

I giggle. "You were the one who insisted on going first."

Sophia throws her dart, but her balloon doesn't have any color either.

"I believe I have this figured out." Paisley pushes her glasses up her nose before marching to the front. She picks up a dart, takes aim, and hits a balloon on the bottom row. It bursts and the color pink explodes.

"I knew it!" I shout before rushing to Nova and throwing my arms around her. "A girl. You're having a girl. I'm so happy for you."

I step back and she wipes tears from her eyes. "I've always wanted a little girl."

I know she has. I'm so happy for her I'm about to burst. Nova is living her own romance novel. She deserves it after losing her parents at such a young age. She deserves all the good things.

"I'm going to spoil your daughter rotten."

"You need to get in line." She thumbs her finger at Hudson. "Daddy is going to spoil his little girl rotten."

Hudson scowls as he marches to us. "Why are you crying?"

The tender way he gazes at Nova has my stomach cramping with envy. I sneak away. I don't want to ruin their moment with my jealousy. I want my friend to have everything she's ever wanted. Including the grumpy resort owner, she claimed to hate. I knew she didn't hate him.

One of Hudson's brothers – I can't tell them apart yet – jumps into the pool and several people join them, including my friends. I don't have my swimsuit on and unlike the other people here, I'm not swimming in my bra and panties.

I find a quiet area to watch the party from. I'm not miserable. I enjoy observing other people having fun.

I'll make sure to remember it all and include it in my next letter to Caleb. I frown. I haven't heard from him in a while. He doesn't write as often as I do but usually, I receive at least one letter a month.

But I haven't gotten a letter this month. And then there's the matter of my latest package being returned to sender. And his phone number no longer being in service.

This has happened before when he's on a mission. But usually, he lets me know in advance. No matter how much I try to convince myself all is well, I'm worried.

Speaking of Caleb, the man leaning against the corner of the chalet could be his twin. Same height. Same bulging muscles. Same blond hair. Same blue eyes.

Hold on a minute. It is Caleb.

"Caleb! You're home!" I shout as I run to him and throw myself at him.

He catches me but immediately sets me back on my feet before retreating. "I knew I shouldn't have come to this party." He turns around and marches away without another word.

What? Why is he being a meanie? I chase after him.

"Caleb. It's me, Maya. Your pen pal," I explain as I try to keep up. He's limping but he's still moving way faster than me. "Slow down."

"Fuck," he mutters before stopping.

"Why are you limping? Are you injured? Is that why you're home? When did you get home? Why didn't you tell me?"

"I didn't tell you because I didn't want to see you."

My eyes widen. "What? Why not?"

"It's not personal."

"Feels pretty personal when you tell me you don't want to see me after twelve years of being pen pals."

He scratches his neck. "I meant I don't want to see anyone."

"Not anyone? What about your family? They've missed you."

He scowls. "My family is better off without me."

"What are you talking about? They're your family. They aren't better off without you. They love you."

Unlike my family who was happy to watch the backside of me walk away. We don't speak. I send birthday cards and Christmas cards but I never receive any cards in return. I can't remember the last time my mother phoned for my birthday.

And I'm not invited to Christmas dinner. Traitors aren't welcome.

"You're better off without me, too."

Pain crashes through my chest at his words. Better off without Caleb? Never. Caleb is everything.

"How about I choose whether I'm better off without you myself? It's this new thing I'm trying out. Being an adult woman and making my own decisions. It agrees with me thus far."

He ducks his chin but not before I notice his lips turn up in a barely there smile.

"I'm trying to protect you."

"Protect me from what? Spending time in real life with the person I've been writing letters to for over a decade?" I narrow my eyes on him. "Or did you ask someone else to write those letters? Have you been pretending to be someone else? Let me guess. You're a super secret spy who's here on a mission because the island has been invaded by aliens."

"Aliens?" He barks out a laugh. "My shy Maya is funny."

"Funny and shy aren't mutually exclusive."

He shakes his head. "Apparently not."

"Come on. Let's go back to the party. Rumor has it they have beer from *Five Fathoms Brewing*, which I have to tell you is the best beer on the island. Not merely the island but in the US. Maybe in the world. I tried to send some to you a few years ago but it's not allowed to send alcoholic beverages to soldiers fighting in Afghanistan, which I learned when some Army dude showed up on my doorstep to ask me if I worked for a terrorist organization."

He scowls. "Who came to your door? Did they scare you?"

"I nearly peed my pants when he asked me if I agreed with Americans being beheaded." I shiver. "Of course, I don't. I don't think anyone should be beheaded. I don't even agree with the death penalty. I know you do. Let's not argue about it now."

"I'll find out who it is and speak to them."

I roll my eyes. "No need to go Rambo on him. He left pretty quick after he noticed all the romance books in my house. He seemed kind of scared."

"You're still obsessed with romance novels?"

"I wouldn't say obsessed. Enamored is the term I'd use."

"Maya!" Paisley shouts. I glance over my shoulder. All of my friends are standing near the chalet watching us.

"I need to go," Caleb says. "Stay safe, Maya."

"That sounds like goodbye!" I shout after him.

"Because it is!"

Silly man. Thinking he can get rid of me. As if. I now have a mission. Find out why Caleb thinks everyone in his life is better off without him. And then convince him he's wrong.

And convince him we're more than friends, a little voice in my mind whispers.

I ignore her. She's delusional from reading too many romance novels. My life is no romance novel.

Chapter 4

"You don't understand shit." ~ Caleb

CALEB

My heart pounds in my chest as I limp back to my cabin. What was I thinking accepting Hudson's invitation? Did I seriously expect Maya not to notice me?

She notices everything. Those whiskey-colored eyes of hers don't miss a thing. I want to watch them flare with passion as I touch every inch of her curvy body. Watch her cheeks darken as I fist her honey blonde hair and expose her neck to me.

I bet her skin tastes like honey. What I wouldn't give to taste her pussy. Drive her mad with desire with my mouth and my fingers before sinking deep into her wet warmth.

My cock hardens and lengthens as images of all the dirty things I've dreamed of doing to Maya over the past decade flirt through my mind.

Damnit! I didn't want her to see me this way. Broken and injured. Hobbling like a damn fawn who hasn't figured out how his legs work yet.

I was supposed to return to Smuggler's Hideaway triumphant. A man who'd proven his worth. Proven I'm good enough for Maya. I snort. Some man I am.

I finally reach the cabin. My left leg is burning from the exertion but I ignore it. If I want to heal and return to the Army, it's going to burn a shitload more before I'm back on active duty.

I enter the cabin and slam the door behind me. I don't bother locking it since I'm in the middle of nowhere.

I collapse on the sofa and bury my face in my hands. For years I've dreamed of my reunion with Maya. She'd run into my arms and I'd kiss those pouty lips I've been fantasizing about for more than a decade. She'd wrap her legs around my waist and I would—

Someone bangs on the door and pulls me out of my fantasy.

"Go the fuck away."

A woman giggles. "He uses the f-word as much as you do." She sounds like Nova.

"What are you doing here?" Hudson asks her.

"I followed you." Yep. It's definitely Nova. Shit. I don't want Maya's friend here. I don't want her seeing me this way and reporting back to Maya.

I growl before pushing to my feet. My leg gives out on me and I crumble to the floor. The door flies open and Hudson rushes in. He reaches for me but I hold up a hand.

"I'm fine."

"Don't look fine to me," Nova quips.

"Nova," Hudson growls. "Now is not the time to be cute."

"Sorry." She sobers. "How can I help?"

"Leave," I grit out.

"I'm not going anywhere when you're laying on the floor."

Hudson grasps her hand. "Sunshine, I'll handle this."

She nibbles on her lip. "But—"

"Promise, Sunshine. I've got this."

"Okay." He kisses her forehead and she walks toward the door.

"Nova," I call and she stops. "Please don't tell Maya about this."

Her brow wrinkles. "Tell Maya about what?"

"About…" I wave my hand toward my leg. My muscles are now shaking from pushing them too far.

"I didn't notice a thing." She winks before shutting the door behind her.

"Can I help you up now?" Hudson asks but doesn't wait for an answer before wrapping his arms around my waist and lifting me into a chair. "Are you sure being out here all alone is a good idea?"

I glare at him. "Don't you start."

He sighs. "I know. I'm a hypocrite. I hid when I returned to the island, too."

"I'm not hiding."

He raises an eyebrow. "And you didn't run like your ass was on fire when Maya approached you either."

"Fuck," I mutter and run a hand through my hair.

He sits on the sofa across from me. "I know we don't know each other well."

Nothing good can follow those words. "No."

"Come on, Caleb. I've been where you are."

"You have?" My nostrils flare as my anger bursts to life. "You know how it feels to nearly be killed loving what you do. To have to drag yourself back home with your tail tucked between your legs. To set eyes on the woman you want but can't have because you're not good enough for her. You know all of it, do you?"

"Yeah, Caleb, I do."

"You know nothing," I snarl.

He holds up his hands. "I get it. I refused to listen to anyone when I returned to Smuggler's Hideaway, too."

"I haven't returned to Smuggler's Hideaway."

His brow wrinkles in confusion. "Um, pretty sure we're on the island now."

"I'm not here permanently."

"You're going to lick your wounds here and then leave? Harsh."

"I'm not licking my wounds."

He raises an eyebrow.

"I'm healing my wounds."

He nods. "Good."

"And then I'm returning to active duty."

He motions to my leg. "With your injury?"

I grit my teeth as another spark of pain erupts in my leg. "Yes."

"Don't you want out? Aren't you done with putting your life in danger?"

I thought I was done. I thought I was ready to return to the island and prove to Maya that I'm the man she wants. But then the enemy showed me I was wrong. I'm not ready yet.

I grunt since I'm not explaining any of my past or present to Hudson. He's only inside this cabin speaking to me now because I'm an idiot who didn't lock my door behind me.

"Message received." He stands and makes his way to the door. He opens it but glances over his shoulder at me before leaving. "The love of a good woman can cure a lot of what's ailing you."

I scowl at him. He doesn't have the first clue what's ailing me. He's a football legend. He doesn't know how it feels to be a nobody. To be told you'll never amount to anything. To be denied the one thing you want in life.

He sighs again before shutting the door behind him.

His visit has taught me one thing. Lock the damn door.

Chapter 5

"It's cute how you think I'll give up." ~ Maya

MAYA

I glance down at the food on my kitchen counter. Fried chicken? Check. Caramel popcorn? Check. Bags of M&Ms? Check. Plus, bread, cheese, and cold cuts.

This should do Caleb for at least a few days. I know he hasn't been going grocery shopping – someone would have seen him and I would have heard about it via the smuggler's grapevine – and he hasn't been getting his groceries delivered. There is no grocery delivery service on Smuggler's Island.

I pack everything into a picnic basket. Time to commence Operation Find Out Why Caleb Thinks Everyone In His Life Is Better Without Him. Step one. Get him to talk to me. Step two. Think of a better name for this operation.

I carry the picnic basket to the car but before I switch on the engine, I check the Where Is Sammy? app. Sammy, the seal, isn't as much of a bother this time of year. When it gets chilly and the tourists don't visit, he tends to behave but it's better to be safe than sorry.

There have been no sightings of him on the road to *Hideaway Haven Resort*. Good. I'm off.

To make things clear, I am not a stalker. Did I snoop around to find out where Caleb is staying? I did. But it's for his own good, which disqualifies me as a stalker.

I turn onto the unpaved driveway leading to Caleb's cabin. Actually, the cabin belongs to Hudson. He bought all of the land surrounding his resort to ensure no one would build a housing settlement nearby. A useless endeavor since the smugglers on the island would never have allowed a housing settlement anyway.

I hit a bump and my head nearly crashes into the ceiling of my car. I slow down to navigate the rest of the way to the cabin.

The tension in my shoulders releases when I reach the cabin and notice a truck parked in front of it and the lights on inside. Caleb's home.

Don't get me wrong. I would have dropped the food off for him regardless of whether he was home or not. But I want to see him. I want to feast my eyes on the man I've been missing for twelve long years. Letters, emails, and the extremely rare Facetime chat are no substitute for the flesh and blood man.

I park in front of the cabin and grab the basket before jumping out of the car and rushing to the front door. The wind off of the Atlantic hits me and I shiver. I should have worn a thicker jacket.

"Caleb!" I shout as I knock on the door. When he doesn't answer, I shout again, "I brought you food and groceries."

I hear footsteps inside the cabin. He's definitely here.

I knock again. "Come on, Caleb. It's cold out here."

"Go home, Maya. I don't want you here."

His words pierce through my heart. I glance down to make sure I'm not bleeding out on his front porch. But there's no actual blood. This pain is not visible. But it exists. Sure as I'm standing here.

If he thinks he can push me away, he's wrong. I'm not giving up. I can't. This isn't the Caleb I know. My pen pal would never turn me away. There's something else going on here. And I will figure it out. I will help Caleb.

"Too bad. I'm here now. Let me in."

"Since when is my shy Maya stubborn?" he grumbles.

"I can be stubborn and shy at the same time."

He doesn't realize it, but with him I'm not shy. I'm not evasive or afraid of crowds or downcast or quiet with him. Caleb makes me feel safe. Makes me feel as if I can say whatever is on my mind. Makes me feel as if he'll protect me if there are too many people crowding me.

"Come on," I cajole. "I have your favorite foods here. Fried chicken, caramel popcorn, M&Ms."

"You know how to tempt a man."

I nearly snort. Me? Maya Jenkins? Tempt a man? Not likely.

The few boyfriends I've had weren't tempted by me. A more accurate description is they thought I'd be easy since I'm quiet and shy. They learned quiet and shy doesn't mean a pushover the hard way since this not-a-pushover knows how to knee a man where it'll hurt the worst.

"I made the chicken right before I came here. It's still hot. I can smell how yummy it is." He doesn't respond but I know he's listening, so I continue, "And the popcorn is caramel. You're favorite."

"You didn't burn it this time?"

"I burned popcorn once in my life. And it wasn't my fault."

"Someone else turned the oven up to the max temperature?"

"I thought it would get done twice as fast if I doubled the temperature."

"It's no wonder you failed home economics."

"Home economics is stupid. It shouldn't be a required class in high school."

"I agree, but at least I was smart enough to not tell the teacher what I thought."

I huff. "I didn't tell Ms. Zimmerman what I thought of Home Ec."

"Of course not. You wrote a letter to the principal outlining why home economics was an element of the male patriarchy and should be stopped."

"I didn't write the letter. Paisley did. And you know it."

"But you signed the letter."

I have no response. Of course, I signed the letter. I was getting a B minus in the class. It was ruining my grade point average. My only shot at attending college without taking out a gazillion student loans was an academic scholarship. B minus does not say academic scholarship.

"Let me in. My arms are getting tired holding this basket."

"You're still refusing to go to the gym to work on your upper body strength?"

Working out is nearly as bad as attending a home economics class. I hate getting all sweaty. I hate all the mirrors reflecting my image at me from every angle imaginable. I hate the way everyone in the gym judges you.

"The only gym on the island is at *Hideaway Haven Resort* and it's too expensive for my blood."

"Too expensive?" I can practically hear the frown in his voice. "I thought *Five Fathoms Brewing* was doing well."

"It's doing better than well. Our beer is officially stocked in grocery stores from Maine to Miami."

Our beer is also why my arms are killing me. I added a six-pack to the bottom of the basket.

"Proud of you, Bunny."

His use of his nickname for me causes a bomb of warmth to explode in my chest. What I wouldn't do for him to use the nickname as a sign of love.

Stop it, Maya. Caleb does not now love you and he never will. He's my friend. Do I want more? Hell, yeah. But Caleb has made it perfectly clear how he feels over the years. And what he feels isn't romantic love. If I didn't know better, I'd say he invented the word friendzone.

"I brought you a six-pack sampler of *Five Fathoms*." I lift up the basket as if to show him but then remember – he's hiding behind a locked door.

"I've tried your beer. It's good."

"You've tried it? When? We can't exactly ship to the Middle East."

He chuckles. "Hudson carries the beer at the resort. And, before you ask, Hudson sent over a care package when I arrived. I didn't go to the resort."

I wasn't going to ask. I admit I'm curious. But I'm not nosy.

Fine. I am nosy. But this is Caleb. The guy who helped me down from the monkey bars in second grade when a group of boys from fifth grade chased me up there.

Climbing up wasn't a problem, but getting back down? Nuh-uh. I wasn't about to climb down. Until Caleb came over and gently showed me how to get down without jumping.

When the fifth grade boys made fun of him for helping the baby, he simply ignored them. It was magnificent. And a crush was born. A crush I've yet to get over. Despite dating other men. Despite nearly two decades passing. The crush lives on.

"Which beer did you enjoy the most? I can bring over a six-pack tomorrow."

He growls and despite knowing the growl is fueled by anger, my body warms and my breasts tingle. This must be how those romance heroines feel in the romances I love to read. Full of anticipation and excitement. Anxious for the next chapter.

"Maya," he grumbles. "You're not hearing me."

"I can hear you just fine. Although, I have to admit, I could hear you better if you opened the door. It's probably warmer inside too. The wind is a cold mistress today."

"Damnit, Maya. You're cold? Get in your car and go home."

Maya this. Maya that. What about Bunny?

I shake those thoughts out of my mind. I'm not Caleb's bunny. Although, my nose is probably pink from the cold. And I am shaking.

"I'm serious, Maya," Caleb says before I can come up with another reason he should let me inside his house. "Leave me alone. I don't want any company."

"Fine. But I'm leaving you the food and you will eat it and enjoy it. Plus, you'll miss me and wish I was here while you're eating."

I set the basket on the porch in front of the door and back up. I wait a minute. Hoping he'll open the door to get the food and I'll get my chance to barge inside but the door stays closed.

Darn it. Caleb has way more patience than me.

"I'm not giving up!" I shout as I hurry down the steps to my car.

I don't bother waiting for Caleb to come out while I'm in my car. He's being extremely stubborn right now.

But there's one thing he didn't count on. I can be more stubborn. Especially when the subject is important. And this subject – making sure Caleb doesn't turn into a hermit – is the most important of all.

I will prove to him the world is not better off without him in it.

My breath seizes in my chest at the thought. I can't imagine a world without Caleb in it. Even if he is halfway across the globe and out of my reach.

Chapter 6

"You haven't begun to experience how stubborn I can be." ~
Maya

Maya

"I need coffee," Sophia moans as we enter the *Pirates Pastries* cafe.

"Lots and lots of coffee," Chloe adds.

Nova groans. "You're mean. You know I can't have coffee."

I guide her toward a table near the window. "You can have coffee in a month after your baby girl is born."

She smiles as she rubs a hand over her large belly. "I can't believe she's almost here."

"I can't believe you bought five bags of clothes for a baby who is going to grow out of them after one wear," Paisley says as she sits next to us.

"How could I resist? The 'I believe in mermaids' t-shirt was too cute to pass up."

Paisley frowns. "Mermaids don't exist."

I wag a finger at her. "They do on Smuggler's Hideaway."

"I can't wait to tell my baby girl all about the mermaid legends."

"You might want to refrain from discussing suicide with your child," Paisley says.

"It's not about the suicide. It's about the love." I sigh. "What's more than romantic than knowing you can't live without the man you love because he drowned in the ocean trying to be with you?"

Paisley wrinkles her nose. "Are you reading mermaid romances now?"

Sophia plops a tray of hot drinks on our table. "I thought you were obsessed with vampire romances."

I roll my eyes. "I wouldn't say obsessed."

Chloe sits down next to me. "You dressed up as a woman with bite marks on her neck and blood dripping down her t-shirt for Halloween."

"I did not," I lie. "Besides, vampires don't cause their mates to bleed."

"You would know all about vampires and their lovers," Parker says as she sets a plate of pastries on our table.

I jump up to hug her. "How are you?"

The owner of the bakery giggles. "You act as if you haven't seen me for months."

"It's been at least a few weeks." A few weeks feels like a long time when you live in a small town where it's normal to bump into every inhabitant at least once a week.

She waggles her eyebrows. "Since you haven't been around because you've been too busy with a certain military hero to stop by for a shipwreck cookie?"

I narrow my eyes on her. "What have you heard?"

She shrugs. "Nothing but you'd be silly to ignore Caleb. He's nearly as hot as Poseidon."

I'm not ignoring Caleb. It's impossible. I swear the man has figured out how to create magnetism since I'm drawn to the cabin he's staying in. It's a force I can't ignore.

"Finally!" Chloe shouts. "I thought we were going to talk about Nova's baby and her baby clothes forever."

Nova wags her finger at her. "You're the one who bought the baby an 'I stop for seals' t-shirt."

"It's tradition. All smugglers should have an 'I stop for seals' t-shirt."

I ignore their argument and nab a Blackbeard's revenge cookie. I moan as the taste of chocolate and peanut butter hits my tongue. I probably shouldn't be eating cookies. I'm curvy enough as it is but who can resist chocolate and peanut butter? Not I.

Chloe leans closer. "Is that how you moan when Caleb touches you?"

Caleb hasn't touched me, but I might have imagined him touching my naked skin a time or two thousand. My cheeks heat, and I duck my chin.

Nova hits Chloe. "Leave Maya alone."

Chloe sweeps a hand over the bakery. "There's no reason to be shy. It's just us in here."

I scan the room. It's Saturday afternoon. Prime bakery goodie eating time but the place is empty except for us. The winter months when tourists don't visit the island are slow but where are the locals?

"I need to get back to the kitchen," Parker says and rushes off before I can ask her if she's in trouble.

Sophia stares after her. "I'm worried about her business. Flynn helped her to renovate the apartment above the bakery for extra cashflow, but there aren't any renters for the winter."

"Maybe we could do some kind of fundraising activity. Smugglers do love their festivals," I suggest.

"Are you going to be in charge?" Paisley asks.

Me? In charge? Of a festival? Talk to all kinds of people and order them around? I'd rather stick my hand in a bee's nest while covered in honey. "I'll handle the money."

"Can we stop with all the delaying now?" Chloe asks. "I kept my mouth shut throughout our shopping trip."

Sophia snorts. "You kept your mouth shut? You wouldn't know how."

"About the Caleb thing. I didn't say a word."

I raise my eyebrows. "You didn't point to the camouflage onesie and ask me if it reminded me of anyone?"

"I didn't say the name Caleb."

She didn't need to. "And you didn't mention how cute 'my little military' baby would look in the onesie?"

"Again, I didn't say the name Caleb."

"Give the girl a cookie. She didn't say Caleb's name."

Chloe beams at me before snatching a cookie from the pile. "Thanks."

"I was being sarcastic."

She winks at me. "I know. Don't care."

"Can we please leave Maya alone now?" Nova asks and I smile at her.

Nova is the only one of my friends who doesn't push me. Who respects my privacy. Although, privacy is a relative word when you live in a small town on a small island where everyone thinks it's *their* business to be all up in *your* business.

"Sorry, Nova. Love you more than my sister, but it's time," Sophia says.

"You don't have a sister," Nova says.

"Thus, why I love you more than my sister."

"Speaking of sisters." Chloe leans closer to Nova. "Do you plan to give this baby girl a sister or a brother?"

"Are you planning to give Natalia a brother or a sister?" Nova fires back at her.

Chloe scowls. "No fair. You know I don't want children."

"And yet you're married and have a step-daughter," Nova says.

Happiness engulfs Chloe's face. The love she has for the family she's created radiates from her. I want that. I want what she has. I want it more than anything. A family. A man to love me. A child to raise.

And I want all of it with Caleb. Blond-haired little boys with blue eyes. They'd be the cutest kids on the island. I know because Caleb was the most adorable little boy on the island until he grew up to be the sexiest man in the world.

Sophia waves a hand in front of my face. "She's dreaming about Caleb."

"Of course, she is," Paisley says as if my daydreaming about Caleb is a foregone conclusion. "She's been dreaming about him since she saw him without a shirt on at the beach when we were teenagers."

"Nope." Nova spins her finger in a rewind motion. "Before then."

"Was it when she let him cheat off her math homework?" Chloe asks.

"You shouldn't let anyone cheat off of you," Paisley says. "It's wrong."

"It was Caleb. She'd give him her last five dollars if he asked for it," Chloe says before leaning in closer. "And? What have you given the military hero lately?" She wags her eyebrows. "A taste of you?"

I shove her away. "Stop. Caleb and I are just friends."

"But everyone on Smuggler's Hideaway knows you want more," Sophia says.

I don't lash out at her since she knows how it feels for the entire island to know who your crush is. And tease you about it. At least, none of the rumors about me ever claimed Caleb rejected me. I wouldn't have handled it very well.

"Doesn't matter," I claim. "Caleb doesn't want me. He doesn't even want to see me."

"I admit he was a bit of a jerk at my baby shower," Nova says. "But he was probably surprised to see you is all. Have you tried to visit him since then?"

"I dropped a basket of food off at his house. He wouldn't even open the door."

She rubs a hand over my back. "I'm sorry, Maya. It was shitty of him, but maybe he has his reasons."

I narrow my eyes on her. "What do you know?"

She shrugs. "Nothing specific, but we all saw the way he was limping when you chased after him."

Thanks for the reminder of how I humiliated myself by chasing after a man who clearly wants nothing to do with me.

"He's obviously suffered a serious injury," Paisley says.

I switch my attention to her. "How do you know?"

"You mentioned he has another two years on his current contract with the Army. He couldn't be hiding away on Smuggler's Hideaway unless he was injured."

I frown. I know Caleb was injured since he was limping. But he was still moving faster than me. I assumed it wasn't a serious injury.

But Paisley has a point. He wouldn't be back home unless he's seriously injured. He's never spent any of his time off on the island before. Why start now?

Hang the mermaids. I'm a horrible person. All I've been thinking about is me and how I'm affected by Caleb's situation when I should be worried about him.

No more mooning over the soldier I can't have.

It's time to be what he needs.

A friend.

Chapter 7

"Whoever said pain is just weakness leaving the body is an asshole who doesn't know shit." ~ Caleb

CALEB

I groan as the muscles in my left leg protest my movement with stabs of pain but I don't stop. I don't quit. I can't. I need to heal from this injury to prove I'm worthy. I lower myself in a squat.

"Hold for five seconds," Hazel orders.

I glare at her as she counts.

"Five, four, three, two, one. And slowly stand."

My body protests as I raise myself into a standing position.

"And again."

"Are you kidding me?"

It feels as if we've been doing therapy for hours. My physical therapist is a sadist.

Hazel bats her eyelashes. "Don't tell me the big bad military hero is tired and needs a rest."

"Not a military hero," I grit out as I lower myself into yet another squat.

"Dude, a bullet shattered your femur during active duty while you were in some godforsaken country you can't talk about. Pretty sure that's the definition of hero."

She doesn't know the whole truth. She doesn't know why I took the bullet. Why I'm not a hero. How I messed up. How I'm a failure. How I battle the guilt every day.

"Not a hero," I grumble.

"Whatever. You can slowly stand now."

My thigh spasms as I push to stand. I grit my teeth and ignore it. It's a squat. I've done a million of these. I can do this. I will do this.

The spasms worsen to convulsions and I lose control of my leg.

"Fuck," I mutter as Hazel wraps an arm around me before I fall.

"I got you, big guy." She helps me to the treatment table and I gladly sit down. "I think you've had enough strength training for the day."

I scowl at her. "You said I could try jogging on the treadmill today."

She wags a finger at me. "No. I said it was a slight possibility. Which I only said because you were super pushy."

"I wasn't pushy."

She giggles. "You haven't changed a bit since high school."

I lift an eyebrow. Granted I was already six foot tall in high school but my frame was lean back then. Now, it's all muscle.

"Yeah. Yeah. Yeah. You've got all these muscles now." She motions to my body as if working my ass off to keep myself in optimum shape is no big deal. "But up here." She taps her temple. "You're the same."

I growl. I am not the same. I was an idiot in high school who thought it was fun to get chased by the cops. It wasn't fun when the principal threatened to fail me if I didn't straighten up.

I'm not an idiot anymore. I have skills. Skills I've honed over twelve years of active duty. Skills that didn't help me when I needed them the most.

Shit. Maybe I am the same. Maybe I'm still the idiot loser I was in high school.

This is why I have to keep Maya at bay. I'm not the man for her. I'm not good enough for her. She deserves more than a man like me who screwed up when it mattered the most.

Hazel taps the treatment table. "Lay down."

"I don't need a fucking nap."

She crosses her arms over her chest and purses her lips. Shame fills me. I'm treating her like the enemy. She's not the enemy. She's trying to help me. Although, it's hard to remember she's helping when her 'help' feels closer to torture.

"Sorry. I'll watch my language."

"Dude. I don't give a shit about your language. Your attitude, though? It could use an adjustment."

"Hard to be all happy go lucky when you're sidelined from active duty."

"As I recall you were never Mr. Happy Go Lucky but I'd love to watch you try." She waggles her eyebrows. "Maybe Maya could help you."

"Don't go spreading rumors about Maya."

She rubs her hands together. "But there are reasons rumors could spread? Awesome. I always thought the two of you would make a cute couple."

This is what happens when you return to your hometown. Everyone knows everybody and is connected somehow. Hazel and I were in the same grade in school together. With Maya and her friends.

"No one thought we'd be a cute couple in high school."

"Wrong." Hazel taps her chest. "I did. I love this."

"Nothing to love. Maya and I aren't together. I don't want to see her. Don't want to see anyone actually."

"Except me."

"Because the Army forced me to."

"Ah. Boo hoo. Is the big bad Army guy afraid of a little therapy?"

She begins to work me through a round of hamstring, quadriceps, and hip flexor stretches.

"Fuck. I thought these stretches were supposed to be gentle."

"Who lied to you?"

She repositions my hip and I grunt at the pain. My hip automatically fights against her but she doesn't have any problem keeping me in position.

"How the hell are you this strong?"

"Farmer's daughter, remember?"

She rattles on as she works me through the stretches. "Dad and Mom were always adamant I work on the farm or at least marry a farmer. Can you say boring? But then my older sister left because she had no interest in living the narrow life they defined for her. After Scarlett left the island and refused to come back, they lightened up a bit and allowed me to go to college. And now Scarlett's back on the island full-time."

"I heard she and Weston are a couple."

Weston wasn't in our class in high school. He was a few years older. But I remember him. Probably because he's the cop who caught me drag racing and threatened to have me jailed until I was too old to drive anymore.

She smiles. "They are. They're totally in love."

I frown. I'm happy for her sister and Weston but I can't help the burn of jealousy in my stomach. Weston has what I want. A loving partner he can spend the rest of his life with. I screwed up any chance I had of being with Maya for the rest of my life.

"I haven't seen you around Smuggler's Rest much. You should totally come to *Smuggler's Cove.* I work at the restaurant in the evenings. We have the best seafood on the island."

I snort. I'm not going anywhere in Smuggler's Rest. I'd stay in my cabin all the time if I could. But when I suggested doing physical therapy there, Hazel pointed out how she needed all the proper equipment if she was going to get me into fighting shape.

She rolls her eyes. "You can't be a hermit forever."

Watch me. I'll be a hermit until the Army declares I'm fit for active duty again. Then, I'm gone from Smuggler's Hideaway and I won't be back.

There's no reason to come back.

Maya always was my reason but I'm not good enough for her. I thought I could become a better man and prove I was good enough for her.

I was wrong.

Chapter 8

"A barnacle ain't got nothing on me" ~ Maya

MAYA

My hands tremble as I set the picnic basket – the picnic basket that magically appeared on my front porch the day after I visited Caleb – in my car.

I'm not scared or nervous about seeing Caleb. I'm anxious and excited.

Okay. Fine. I am a bit nervous about asking him why he's here on Smuggler's Hideaway. I'm a fool for not realizing he could be badly injured.

I was being totally selfish, thinking only about myself. Why doesn't Caleb want to see me? Is he mad at me? What did I do wrong? All me, me, me.

But Nova's right. There's something else at play here. Caleb hasn't come home in over a decade and now he shows up for a bit of rest and relaxation? Except he's hiding in a cabin in the woods. And he's limping. Something's wrong and it's time I figured out exactly what.

I switch on my car and drive to his cabin.

I am doing the right thing, I reassure myself as I drive. *Caleb is my friend. He needs help and I'm helping him.*

This is exactly what a heroine in a romance novel would do. She wouldn't stay home and cower in the corner while the man she loves needs her. She'd rush to his rescue.

Romance novels are the best. Too bad I'm not in the middle of one. Caleb would make an awesome hero. Military heroes are beyond sexy. Unfortunately, we're just friends.

I arrive at the turnoff for Caleb's cabin and slow down. The driveway is unpaved and bumpy. I don't want his beer to get all shook up.

His truck is parked in front of the cabin. Good. He's here.

Ha! Did I actually think he wouldn't be? No one's spotted Caleb in town yet. I might be keeping my ear to the ground for any rumors involving him.

Thus far, the only rumors are speculations about how long he's staying. I wouldn't be surprised if the inhabitants of Smuggler's Hideaway are already betting on when he'll leave.

I park next to his truck and haul the basket out of the car. It's heavier this time since Caleb mentioned he enjoys *Five Fathoms Brewing*. He didn't say which beer he preferred so I got him an extended variety pack.

I trudge up the stairs and set the basket on the porch near the door before knocking. Twelve beers is too heavy for me to hold onto while I wait for Caleb to open the door.

"Caleb! It's me Maya!"

"Go away. I'm not in the mood."

"Not in the mood for what? Delicious food? Yummy beer? Awesome company? You'll have to narrow things down for me."

"Not in the mood," he repeats.

"Is that an all of the above answer? You know if you're guessing all of the above is not the best answer to choose."

"Not guessing."

I ignore his response and plow forth. "Remember when I used to tutor you in math? You never could sit still long enough for me to explain the Pythagorean theory. Paisley claims I let you cheat. But I didn't. You completed those math tests all on your own."

I pause and wait for him to respond. To engage in some manner. The last time I was here he wouldn't open the door but we did have a bit of a chat.

I wait some more but apparently, he's not going to engage today.

Moving on to Plan B. The plan where I stop making it all about me.

"Caleb, are you okay? Nova said you're injured."

He stomps to the door but he doesn't open it. "What the hell did Nova say?"

His obvious anger has me backtracking. "She didn't give me any details. She merely pointed out how you wouldn't be on Smuggler's Hideaway if something wasn't wrong. After all, you haven't visited since you left."

My heart squeezes. We're friends and yet he never bothered to visit me over the past decade. His family met up with him in various places for holidays but I was never invited. He never even told me about those visits. I found out via the smuggler's grapevine.

"Caleb." I place my hand on the door. I wish I could touch him. Hold him in my arms and comfort him but he won't let me. He won't even open the door. "Are you okay?"

"Fucking fabulous."

I frown. High school Caleb swore here and there. Mostly to be a rebellious teen. But grown-up Caleb swears like a sailor. Or a soldier, I should say.

"I don't believe you."

"Are you saying I'm a liar, Mouse?"

How dare he call me mouse? Friends are not assholes to each other. And I won't stand for it. I'm shy, not a pushover.

"Do not call me Mouse! You hear me. I am not a mouse."

Mouse is the nickname the bullies in school used. Mostly, I ignored them. Bullies lose their power when they're ignored.

But sometimes they'd corner me in the hallway at school. Surrounded by a crowd of people with a group of boys encircling me is my personal nightmare. A few times Caleb saved me from those bullies. He knows exactly how I feel about the name mouse.

"Sorry, Mouse."

I slam my hand against the door. "Damnit, Caleb. You can't apologize for calling me mouse by calling me mouse again."

"What do you want from me?"

"I don't want anything from you."

"Liar."

Who is this asshole? This isn't the Caleb I know. The one who saved me from bullies. The one who's written me letters – real letters, not emails – for the past decade. The one who sent me a surprise gift for my twenty-first birthday – a turquoise bracelet I wear all the time.

"I want to help you."

He snorts. "By helping yourself."

"How am I helping myself? I brought you a basket of food and I'm worried about you. This isn't about me."

"There's no need to worry about me."

"Then, why won't you open this door? Why won't you let me inside? Why can't we speak face-to-face? Why do you think everyone in your life is better off without you?"

"Why? Why? Why? It's all about Maya."

I stop myself before I shout in response. Shouting through the door at each other is not getting us anywhere. Although, it may keep me warm out here.

"I'm trying to understand why my friend I haven't seen in over a decade doesn't want to spend any time with me."

"I told you. You're better off without me."

"Let me be the judge of that."

"Too late. I already adjudicated the matter and the verdict is clear."

I giggle. There's my Caleb. Being silly and funny. He used to make me laugh out loud all the time when I was tutoring him in the library. The librarian threatened to kick us out on a daily basis.

"I want to appeal."

"Sorry. No appeal is possible in this matter."

"Okay." I try a different angle. "Can you explain why?"

"Nope. Trust me. You're better off not knowing."

"Do you think I can't handle it? I can handle lots of things. I spent half of high school in detention for things my friends did. And I never complained. Never tattled on them."

"What your friends did? You never participated?"

"Being a lookout is not the same thing as committing the crime of breaking and entering."

"The law would disagree with you there."

He's probably right. I've never researched the matter. Better not to know in my opinion.

"Open the door and I'll tell you all about the time we broke into the principal's office."

I hear him sigh on the other side of the door. "You're not hearing me, Maya. I'm not opening this door. I don't want to see you."

"Why not?"

"None of your damn business."

I flinch at how cruel his words sound.

"I'm your friend."

"Doesn't mean you have the right to know everything about me."

"But I know literally nothing. Not why you're here. Not how long you're staying. Nothing. I'm out here in the dark."

"Here's a suggestion. Hop in your car and switch on the lights before driving back to Smuggler's Rest."

"Caleb. Don't send me away," I practically beg. I'm not too proud to beg when it comes to Caleb. I'd do anything for him. Except leave him alone when he needs me. That I won't do.

"Damnit, Maya. I don't want you here. I don't know how else to say it except leave and don't come back."

My eyes itch and tears well at his words. "Why are you doing this to me, Caleb?"

"I'm not doing shit to you. Leave, Maya."

I give in. Today is obviously not the day he's going to open the door to me. I might as well go away and get warm back home. But I won't leave him alone forever.

"I'll be back."

"Don't come back, Maya. Leave me alone. I'm serious. I don't want to see you. Not now. Not tomorrow. Not ever."

Tears flow down my cheeks at his words. I know he's hurting and this isn't him speaking but his words still hurt.

But I'm not giving up. I do not give up on my friends. No matter how much they try to push me away. I will be a barnacle on his back.

Watch him try and push me away.

Chapter 9

"It's not real. No matter how much I wish it were." ~ Caleb

CALEB

I grit my teeth as I grasp the edge of the bathtub and haul myself out of the water using my upper body. According to Hazel, taking an ice bath after her torture sessions is supposed to help with muscle recovery and alleviate soreness. All this bath has helped is to freeze my balls off.

I sit on the edge of the bath and wrap myself in a towel. I avoid looking at my leg. The scars and puckered, red skin remind me of things I don't want to remember.

Once I'm dry, I don some sweats and hobble to the kitchen. Hazel wants me to use a cane after our sessions but I refuse. I'm not a cripple.

My stomach growls. I wonder if I have any casserole left from Maya.

Maya. I'm such an asshole. I hate how she left here crying the other day. I had to lock down every single muscle in my body to stop myself from going after her. She doesn't get it. She doesn't understand. She is better off without me.

I can barely handle myself these days. I'm not the man she needs. I glare down at my leg. I'm hardly a man at all.

Light reflects off the kitchen window and I growl. Someone's driving down the road to the cabin.

I am not in the mood for visitors. Especially not after a grueling physical therapy session.

I make my way to the living room window and peek outside. Maya is climbing out of her car. The wind picks up her honey blonde hair and it flies around her head. She tugs on a pink knit hat before reaching inside her car.

I groan at the sight of her perfect ass bent over. How I wish I could dig my fingers into her hips while I bend her over my sofa and bury myself inside her wet heat. I bet she'd go wild for me. Maya is shy but there's a hint of wild in there. I witnessed it for myself the one time I touched her lips.

She stands and she's now holding a picnic basket. I growl. Damn picnic basket.

No matter how many times I send Maya away, she returns with a picnic basket of food for me. Casseroles she took the time to make for me. Cookies she took the time to bake for me.

Doesn't she realize I'm a lost cause? She shouldn't be spending her precious time on me.

She straightens her back before marching up the steps to the front door of the cabin. People – especially assholes in high school – assume shy little Maya is timid and afraid. She's the furthest thing from timid. She's brave and loyal and fucking perfect.

Evidence of her marching back here to feed me after I was a complete dick to her last time and made her cry. I rub a hand over my chest at the ache the thought of her tears creates.

"Caleb!" she shouts as she knocks on the door.

"Go away, Bunny."

The nickname Bunny slips out. I shouldn't use it. I shouldn't give her hope that we can rekindle our friendship in person since I'm home.

Because I'm not home. This is temporary. A bump in the road. As soon as my leg is healed, I'll be back on active duty and a million miles away from here.

"If you didn't want me to stop by with more beer and food, you shouldn't have brought my picnic basket back to me."

Crap. I knew returning her picnic basket would give her the wrong idea but I couldn't keep it. Having a possession of Maya's in the cabin was too big of a temptation. The sight of the picnic basket taunted me. Made me question my reasons for not pursuing her, for shutting her out. Which is the last thing I needed.

"How do you know I returned the picnic basket? Maybe I asked someone else to do it."

She barks out a laugh. "Silly man. If you didn't want to get caught, you shouldn't have insisted I get a doorbell camera."

Damn. I forgot all about her camera. I should have left the picnic basket on the back porch. But I didn't want to look like a damn stalker creeping through her yard.

"I made your favorite," she sings. "Irish beef stew using *Five Fathoms Brewing Depth Charge Stout*."

My mouth waters. I love Irish beef stew. And I bet it's even better using the stout beer from her brewery. The *Five Fathoms* beers are awesome. The last time I met my parents in Germany for the holidays I made them bring me a bunch of it.

I nearly reach for the door but I fist my hand when I remember. I can't be a good friend to Maya. She deserves better than a broken man who's a failure.

"I'm not opening the door, Maya." I don't know who I'm trying to convince – me or her?

"You can't out stubborn me, Caleb Emerson."

"Pretty sure I can, Maya Jenkins."

"Ha! Remember the time the principal pitted us against each other? He was determined to find out who stole the Rogue's Landing's mascot. For some reason, he thought I might have had something to do with the missing raccoon."

"Because you did, Maya."

She ignores me to continue her story. "She sat us in his office and told us we couldn't move until one of us confessed. It wasn't me who confessed."

I growl. "I told her what I knew because you were squirming in your chair. I was afraid you were going to pee your pants."

She gasps. "I would never."

"Which is why you ran to the girl's restroom faster than lightning the second I confessed."

"Oh please. If I could run faster than lightning, I would have been on the track team. But they wouldn't even let me try out for the team. I believe their words were, 'you're not fast enough to carry our water for us'."

"Those kids were assholes."

"Totally. I appreciate you stealing all of their shoes so they couldn't compete in their first track meet."

"I didn't steal their shoes." I totally did. They deserved it. They knew Maya was under my protection but they didn't heed my warnings. I showed them what happens when they ignore me.

"Sure, you didn't. And you didn't..."

Her voice trails off. "Didn't what?"

"We have company."

Company? I didn't hear anyone drive down the road. I hurry to the living room window. My parents are climbing out of their minivan.

They promised they wouldn't come here anymore. They said they'd give me time. I guess my time is up. Crap.

"Hi, Mrs. Emerson." Maya greets Mom with a hug.

"Son, are you in there?" Dad shouts.

I can't exactly ignore my parents and pretend I'm not home when Maya's standing on the porch, obviously talking to me. Mom will lose her mind. She did her best to teach me how to be a gentleman.

I open the door and Maya forces her way past me. She saunters to the kitchen and places her basket on the counter as if she belongs here.

"A picnic basket?" Mom claps her hands. "How romantic."

Maya's eyes widen and her cheeks darken.

"We're not—"

I don't get a chance to finish. "I'm glad you have someone to help you around while you're injured."

I scowl at Mom. Maya isn't supposed to know how injured I am. To Maya's credit, she doesn't flinch or act surprised.

"He doesn't need my help. Except with cooking. We all know how bad a cook he is."

"I always knew the two of you were destined to be together." Mom sighs. "You're adorable together."

"Wait. What?" I ask.

"There's no need to hide from us, Son," Dad says.

"I'm not hiding."

Mom rolls her eyes. "We haven't seen you since you got home. We only know you go to physical therapy three times a week because I ran into Hazel at *Smuggler's Cove.*"

I glance at Maya but she doesn't act surprised by the information. I frown. Does everyone on Smuggler's Hideaway know about my injuries? I dismiss the thought. Maya wouldn't be here begging me for answers if she knew.

"I'm glad you're not hiding from your girlfriend," Mom continues to babble away.

I should correct Mom. Tell her Maya hasn't even been inside my cabin until five minutes ago.

But maybe if my parents believe I'm dating Maya, they'll stop bothering me. Being left alone is what I want most.

Except to spend time with Maya.

Hold on. This is the perfect way to spend time with Maya without leading her on. We can pretend to date. My parents will be happy. And I can spend some time with Maya. And when I'm all healed up, I can drive away from this island without anyone getting hurt.

Maya raises an eyebrow at me. I know her well enough to understand the question she's asking. Does she roll with it or deny it?

I give her a subtle nod before raising my arm. She hurries to me and buries herself in my side. She fits perfectly against me. As if she were made for me. I inhale her honey scent and calm spreads over me.

This is where she belongs. If I were a better man, I'd never let her leave my side.

Unfortunately, I'm not a better man. I left over a decade ago to prove I could be the man for her, but I did the exact opposite. I proved I'm not good enough for her.

"Well," Dad says and brings me out of my reverie. "We'll leave you two alone. Your mother just wanted to check on you."

Mom elbows him. "Don't lie. You were worried, too."

He grins down at her. "Yes, dear."

My parents are still in love. Five children later and they continue to stare at each other with cartoon hearts in their eyes. I want what they have.

I glance down at Maya. Those whiskey-colored eyes are full of warmth and her pouty lips are tipped up in a smile at me. If I were a better man, I could meld my lips to hers.

I've never wanted to be a better man more than in this moment.

Chapter 10

"Fake date Caleb? I'll fake date him all the way to real." ~
Maya

MAYA

I wave to Caleb's parents as they drive away. Caleb has his arm firmly wrapped around me and I'm melted into him. His earthy scent with undertones of spice surrounds me and I want to stay in this moment forever.

But I can't.

Caleb didn't even want me inside his cabin before his parents showed up. He definitely doesn't want to be my boyfriend. We're friends. Nothing more. Except for the one time in the library.

I slam my walls down before the memory invades my consciousness. The last thing I need to do is embarrass myself in front of my high school crush.

"Welp," I say when the lights from his parents' car can no longer be seen. "I guess it's time to stage a break-up."

He frowns down at me. "A break-up?"

I roll my eyes. "You know. A break-up. As in what happens when a 'couple' no longer wants to be together."

"You want to break up with me?"

I giggle. "We're not dating, Caleb. We faked it for your mom, remember? Or did you get a head injury?" I pause. "Oh shit. Do you have a head injury? I was joking but is that why your mom was happy you have someone around while you're injured? Do I need to get you inside? Should you be standing?"

I try to lead him inside but he growls. "I don't have a head injury."

"Phew." I drag the back of my hand over my forehead. "I was freaking out there for a minute."

A minute? Snort. I've been freaking out since the moment Nova mentioned Caleb could be seriously injured.

He drops his arm and motions to the door. "We should probably discuss this inside."

Inside? I clamp down my muscles before I jump for glee. Caleb is letting me inside his cabin when his parents aren't around. Take that, progress! I'm winning today.

I stroll into the cabin as if I'm not jumping for joy on the inside. *Be cool, Maya.* I've never been cool in my life but today is a great day to start.

"Have a seat."

I sit on the sofa and wait for Caleb to join me. He doesn't. He paces back and forth in front of me. He's obviously limping and in pain. There are brackets around his mouth.

"Caleb." I pat the sofa next to me. "You should sit down."

"I don't need to sit."

Ah, big macho Caleb has arrived at the party. I let him be. I learned long ago you can't win against a macho man.

"Okay. What do you want to discuss? If it's about the break-up, I can break up with you. I'll tell everyone I dumped you because you didn't perform in bed."

He chuckles and his dimple comes out. A dimple I want to trace with my tongue. How does his skin taste? How does it feel? I've imagined it a million times but I bet the real thing is better than my imagination. And I have a stellar imagination.

"You wouldn't dare tell everyone in Smuggler's Hideaway I can't perform in bed."

I cross my arms and narrow my eyes at him. "Oh yeah? Try me."

He frowns. "You're not telling anyone I can't perform in bed since we're not breaking up."

I scratch my neck. "We're not? You do realize we're not actually dating, right?"

He sits on the coffee table in front of me. "I know. And I know I'm no prize."

I rear back. "No prize? I'd like to revisit the idea of you having suffered a head injury."

"I don't have a head injury. But my leg is screwed."

I reach for his hands and he squeezes mine. I'm too worried to enjoy the warmth of touching him. "How bad is it? What happened? Are you okay?"

"I'm okay. The injury is bad, but I'm working with a therapist and doing my exercises. I won't always walk with a limp like some loser."

"Some loser? Do you think of yourself as a loser? You get injured protecting this country and you're a loser? Maybe I should have tutored you in English as well as Math."

He squeezes my hands once more before releasing me. I immediately miss his warmth.

"Don't make me out to be a hero."

"It's official. I definitely should have tutored you in English. Thus far, you don't understand the definition of loser or hero. Those are pretty basic words. Are you certain you passed English class in high school?"

He grunts. "I passed English. And I'm done talking about this."

"But you never told me how you got your injury. What happened? How bad is it?"

"Need to know," he grunts.

I let it go. After a decade of being pen pals, I'm intimately acquainted with the words 'need to know'.

I hold up my hands. "I'm officially letting it go." For now.

"Moving on. Let's discuss dating."

My heart skips a beat. Dating. What I wouldn't do to date Caleb. He's my dream man. Has been for decades. But we're friends. He shoved me into the friend zone when he shipped out to basic training immediately after our high school graduation.

"We're friends, remember?"

Ugh. I hate the word friends where Caleb is concerned. Don't get me wrong. I think it's important for a couple to be friends. But 'only friends'? Ugh. No thanks.

"My family's worried about me."

My head spins from the change of subject but I roll with it. "Why?"

He scowls. "Let's just say they haven't seen much of me since I returned to the island."

In other words, he's hiding from everyone. Not just me.

"Why are you hiding from your parents? They love you."

Acid churns in my stomach. A big, gaping hole exists in my life where my family should be. I would give up all my romance books for my parents to love me. Instead, they've rejected me time and time again. They ignore me and pretend I don't exist.

Caleb doesn't respond so I keep going. "And your sisters love you, too. They miss you. They want to spend time with you."

He smiles and his dimple comes out again. How he can look so rugged and cute and adorable at the same time is a mystery to me, but he pulls it off.

"Willow, Abigail, Clara, and Eliza are crazy."

I don't disagree. I don't really know his sisters. But I'd love it if they were my sisters. I'd love any siblings but my mom couldn't have children after me. Not after my dad—

I shove those thoughts away. I'm not thinking about my parents now. Caleb needs me. He deserves my attention. Not them.

"What I'm trying to say…" He pauses.

"Yes?"

"I think we should fake date to stop my family from worrying about me."

It's a good thing I'm sitting because his words would have knocked me off my feet if I were standing. Holy mermaids! He wants to date me.

Fake date, I correct myself.

Whatever. Fake dating still means spending time with him. It means he's not embarrassed to be seen with me. The girl with more curves than the ocean has waves.

I inhale a deep breath and calm myself before I jump him. We're merely pretending to date. Pretending to date doesn't mean I get to strip his clothes off and lick every inch of him.

Wait a smuggler minute! Does fake dating mean those things? I read romance novels. I know all about how couples fake date in public but get busy in the sheets in private. What does Caleb want?

"Define fake dating."

"We'll pretend to be a couple in front of my family."

"How is this supposed to work? You just admitted you're avoiding your family."

He grunts. "There's no way I can avoid them any longer. Especially not when they think you're in the picture."

My stomach warms. I'm in the picture. Little old me.

"Okay. How does this work?"

"Simple. Whenever I'm forced to meet my family, you come with and act as my buffer."

I'll be his buffer whenever he needs it. I'll be whatever he needs from me.

I should probably set ground rules about touching and kissing. It's what a romance heroine would do.

But I'm no fool. If Caleb wants to break the 'fake dating' rules and kiss me or touch me, I won't say no.

I stick out my hand. "You have a deal."

He reaches for my hand but I draw mine away. He raises an eyebrow.

"And you'll open the door when I come by with a care package from now on."

I stick out my hand again. He hesitates.

"Promise you won't come every night."

Dang. He figured me out. I'd be here every night playing girlfriend if he'd let me.

I roll my eyes. "I have a very busy life. I don't have time to be here every night."

Lies. Lies. Lies.

He places his hand in mine. It engulfs mine and makes me feel tiny. It's a new feeling. I like it. More than like it if I'm being honest. But apparently, honesty is not my thing at the moment.

"We have a deal."

I can't help the smile from crossing my face. This is going to be awesome. I get to spend time with my crush and there will be no more doors shut in my face.

You should protect your heart.

I ignore my inner voice. She doesn't know what she's talking about.

Chapter 11

"Trust me. Things can always get worse." ~ Caleb

CALEB

"I'm sorry about this," I tell Maya as we make our way to the restaurant.

I tug on my collar. I feel as if every single person in downtown Smuggler's Rest is staring at me. My body tingles with heat at all of their eyes on me.

Maya squeezes my hand and calm settles over me. She has the ability to quiet my mind with a single touch. Too bad I can't keep her.

"Don't be sorry. I'm getting a free meal out of this."

We reach *Smuggler's Cove* and I drop her hand to open the door to the restaurant. I guide her inside with a hand on her lower back. She shivers at my touch. I wonder how she'd respond if I touched her naked skin. Would she shiver and beg me for more?

My cock twitches. It's on board with finding out exactly how Maya would respond. It's tired of using my hand for sexual relief.

Hazel waves at me and I force my thoughts away from Maya naked. I'm not getting hard in front of my physical therapist.

"You made it! I didn't think anything other than meeting me could get you out of the house." Hazel opens her arms for a hug and Maya growls. It's barely audible but I hear it.

Is my little bunny jealous? I glance down at her and she's throwing daggers out of her eyes at Hazel. I wrap an arm around her to make my allegiance clear. She cuddles into me.

Hazel drops her arms at my display. "Awesome. You two are finally together!"

Maya's shoulders relax and the tension drains out of her. I lean down to whisper in her ear. "Hazel is my physical therapist."

Her eyes widen and she opens her mouth – probably to fire questions at me – but my parents and sisters arrive before she has the chance.

"You ready for this?" I ask.

"Are you ready for this?" she fires back at me.

"You're here!" Mom's shout has the entire restaurant whipping around toward the door to find out who spoke.

I gulp. I'm not imagining things now. Everyone is staring at me. Wondering what Caleb is doing home. Wondering why I'm limping. Wondering how I incurred my injuries. Wondering how I screwed up.

Maya places a hand on my cheek. "Hey." I draw my gaze to hers and she smiles. "I'm here. I'm not going anywhere."

I might have made Maya promise not to abandon me at the restaurant before we left my cabin. I was worried about my family grilling me with questions. But, apparently, my family is the least of my problems. I didn't count on how it'd feel to have all the inhabitants of the island staring at me.

I refuse to respond to their stares. I can handle this. I've handled much worse and came out fine. My leg twinges to remind me 'fine' is a relative word.

I nod at Maya and she drops her hand. I immediately miss the feel of her soft skin against mine. I want to drag her hand back. I want to feel her hands everywhere on my body. I want to inhale her honey scent into my lungs as she touches me.

My cock twitches again. I'm surprised by the jolt of sexual awareness. Seconds ago, I was ready to flee the restaurant but now I'm ready to throw Maya over my shoulder and run out of the restaurant to somewhere private where I can devour her. This woman makes me crazy.

"Caleb." Maya squeezes my hand. "Hazel is showing us to our table."

I clear my throat and force thoughts of Maya naked away. Again. "Lead the way."

She studies my face for a moment before nodding. She follows my parents and sisters to a table in the corner. It's not secluded but at least people won't be walking past us constantly. Using the location of the table as an excuse to spy on me.

Dad settles himself in the seat in the corner with his back to the wall and my hands begin to tremble. I can't sit with my back exposed to everyone in the restaurant. I'll be vulnerable to an attack I won't see coming.

"Mr. Emerson," Maya speaks softly and no one hears her. "Mr. Emerson." She speaks loud enough for half the restaurant to hear her. Her cheeks darken and sweat forms on her brow but she continues.

"Do you mind if I sit in the corner with Caleb? I'm feeling a bit cold and want to avoid any draft."

My brow wrinkles. Does Maya know I want to sit in the corner? I don't get the chance to ask her before everyone shuffles around until we're seated in the corner with my parents across from us and my sisters on either side.

"Better?" Maya whispers to me once everyone's situated.

"How did you know?" I ask since there's no denying she knows I was panicking about sitting with my back to the people in the restaurant.

She shrugs. "I read."

"Now Maya," Mom begins before I have a chance to question Maya further. "Tell us all about how Caleb and you started dating. My son hasn't told me a thing."

Maya's cheeks darken once again. I can't help but wonder how far her blush goes. Does it reach her breasts? Are her nipples a pretty pink to match her lips?

My cock hardens and lengthens at the idea of those pretty pouty lips on my hard length. I clear my throat and adjust myself under the table. At least we're sitting and no one can notice the result of my inappropriate thoughts.

"Um." Maya nibbles on her lips. She is not helping the situation in my pants at all.

Her gaze catches mine. Shit. Those whiskey-colored eyes aren't full of want and need. She's panicking. The attention of five women – my four sisters and Mom – and my dad is too much for her. Especially when we're in a crowded restaurant.

I'm an asshole. I should have realized this evening would be a lot for her and protect her. Instead of spending all my time being a horndog. The night's not over yet.

I wrap an arm around her shoulders. "There's not much to tell. We've been friends forever and she finally agreed to give me a chance."

"You wore her down? Good tactic." My sister, Willow, nods in approval.

Which reminds me. "Have you met my sisters, Maya?"

"Not officially," she mutters since everyone knows of everyone else on the island.

I point to Willow. "This is Willow. Next to her is Abigail." I point to the other side of the table. "And this is Clara and Eliza."

Maya waves to everyone. "Hi." When her shy side comes out, she's absolutely adorable.

The waitress arrives and hands out menus.

"Awesome. I'm starving," Abigail says as she grabs a menu.

A cheer sounds in the bar area and I jump in my chair. I search for the cause of the disruption. It's just a hockey game showing on the televisions hung up around the bar. The favorite team probably scored.

I inhale a deep breath and allow my heart rate to return to normal. There's no threat here. I'm having dinner with my family and Maya. There's no reason to panic.

"I think I'll have the Smuggler's Meatloaf," Maya says. "What are you having?"

Another cheer erupts in the bar area. I lock my muscles before I flinch again. I'm on Smuggler's Hideaway. No insurgents are hiding in plainclothes to try and shoot me or plant an IED. I'm safe.

Another cheer and I jump from my chair. Panic coursing through my veins. My hands tremble and I can't catch my breath. I feel nauseous and my chest aches.

I need to get out of here. I need to find cover. I need to get to safety.

Maya grabs my hand and pulls me away from the table. "Come on. This way." She leads me into a room and shuts the door behind us. I fall to my ass on the floor as my heart races.

"Name five things you can see."

I glance up at Maya but I can't make out her features since my vision is blurry. "What?"

"Five things. Name them."

I blink to clear my vision and glance around the room. "Shelves. Floor. Lightbulb. Door. You."

"Good." She nods. "Four things you can touch."

I touch my face. "Nose, mouth, ears, cheeks."

"I think you're cheating, but I'll allow it."

Cheating? How am I cheating?

"Three things you can hear."

"I hear you. I hear people in the bar."

"What else do you hear?"

She taps her toes and I point to her foot. "You. Tapping your foot."

"Two things you can smell."

I inhale a deep breath and try to make out the scents of the restaurant. "Pizza and honey."

"Honey?" She frowns. "I don't smell honey."

I shrug. "You always smell of honey to me."

"One thing you can taste."

I'm confused. Am I supposed to be eating now?

She hands me a breadstick.

"Did you steal this breadstick?"

"It's not my fault they didn't lock the storeroom."

I bark out a laugh and realize I can breathe. I can see. I can hear. My panic has subsided and my chest is no longer tight.

Damnit. I didn't want Maya to witness me having a panic attack. It's one of the reasons I've stayed away from her. I don't want her to think I'm pathetic. But now she will. After the way I panicked because some stupid hockey team scored and people in the bar cheered.

I run a hand through my hair. "Maybe—"

Maya holds up a hand. "Nope."

"What? Nope?"

"You're not going to sit there and apologize for having a panic attack. It's plain stupid."

"Stupid?"

"Yes." She nods. "Stupid."

"I'm stupid for having a panic attack?"

She glares at me. "No. You're human for having a panic attack. You're stupid if you're going to apologize and beat yourself up for having one."

"You see right through me."

"Duh. We're friends. Friends know and understand each other."

"Nonetheless, I should be the one protecting you." She shouldn't be forced to be in this room with me, talking me down from a panic attack.

"I didn't know there were rules about who protects whom."

"I bet in your romance books the hero always protects the woman."

"Who says I need protecting?"

She holds out her hand. I contemplate it for a second. I could ignore it but I can't stand from this position without help. Not yet at least.

I grasp her hand and she helps me to stand. Her hand feels right in mine.

Maybe I was wrong to push Maya away. It's obvious she can handle my broke ass. Maybe it's time to finally declare what I've always known is true.

Maya is mine.

My thigh twinges.

Or maybe not.

Chapter 12

"Bullies are jerks but do they tell the truth? Asking for a friend."
~ Maya

MAYA

I shut the dishwasher and make sure it starts before digging my phone out of my pocket. I glance around to make sure no one's watching me, but there's no one else in the restaurant kitchen at the moment.

It's Saint Patrick's Day and it's all hands on deck at *Five Fathoms Brewing.* I don't care how busy we get. I am not working the bar or restaurant floor. There are way too many people out there. It's hot and loud and crowded.

I shiver. No way.

Which is why I'm on dishwashing duty all night. The dishwasher behind the bar is not enough to keep up with a Saint Patrick's Day crowd, which is why I'm in the kitchen. But since there's a lull in the dishes, I decide to message Caleb.

How did therapy go?

He responds right away.

How do you know I had therapy?

Hazel's easy to bribe. One pirate's plunder muffin and she caved.

What did she say?

I need to be careful here. It's obvious Caleb has some shame attached to his injuries, which makes no sense. But I know all about people being ashamed for things they should be proud of, so I tread carefully.

You had therapy today. Oh, and you swear like a sailor.
I'm not a sailor.
I know but I couldn't resist the chance to tease you.
I'll show you teasing.
Promises. Promises.

What am I doing? I'm not supposed to flirt with my fake boyfriend. This madness will end in heartbreak. I've read the romance books. I know how this goes.

I always keep my promises.

Hold on. He's not supposed to flirt back with me. How do I respond? Do I continue to flirt? What do I write? A message pops up before I can figure out how to reply.

Do you want to come over for dinner tomorrow night? I want to thank you for taking care of me in the restaurant.
There's no need to thank me.
I decide when I thank someone.
And you've decided, have you?
Come to dinner tomorrow night.

Does he think he has to persuade me? Of course, I'm going to say yes. As if I would ever say no to Caleb. I don't think my body is capable of saying no to the man.

What time? And what do you want me to bring?

I have everything covered. Bring yourself.

The door slams open and Chloe rushes in carrying a tray of dirty glasses.

Gotta go. See you tomorrow.

I stuff my phone in my back pocket.

"I got it," I say as I accept the tray from Chloe.

She brushes the hair off of her forehead. "It's crazy out there. I've never seen it this busy."

I snort. "What did you think would happen when you came up with a bunch of games with beer prizes?"

Smugglers are competitive enough. Add in a beer prize and they go absolutely all out nuts. Naturally, all of the games are rowdy, too. There's a tug-of-war between smugglers and mermaids, a mermaid storytelling contest, and the best mermaid-inspired cocktail contest.

"I honestly didn't think people would dress up as smugglers and mermaids and spend the entire night before the tug-of-war daring each other to drink."

I giggle. "I don't know why not. It's exactly what you would have done."

She shrugs. "True."

The dishwasher beeps to let me know it's finished. I open it and Chloe grabs the tray of glasses.

"Thanks." She rushes away but spins around before she reaches the door. "You okay in here by yourself?"

My brow furrows. "Why wouldn't I be okay?"

"It's a party out there and you're in here."

"And?"

"Flynn and Lucas are here, too."

"And Nova and Hudson are home because she just had her baby." They named her Iliana. The name is derived from the Greek word *ilis*, meaning bright. It's the perfect name since Hudson's nickname for Nova is Sunshine. "What's your point?"

"I feel bad you're all by yourself."

"You feel bad? Are you sick? Do I need to phone the doctor? Wild child Chloe is worried about someone else's feelings."

She glares at me. "I worry about other people."

I know she does. She used to hide how she cared about other people, but Lucas and his daughter Natalia have changed her. I'm happy for her. I'm also a bitch for trying to steer the subject away from my own preference for being alone.

"Sorry."

"Chloe!" someone shouts from the bar area.

"Shit. I need to go. Promise me you'll let me know if you want some company."

I don't hesitate since I know I won't want any company. The only company I want is a man who prefers to hide away in his cabin all alone. He'll probably become more of a hermit after the restaurant incident. He's got another thing coming if he thinks I'll let him hide.

"Promise."

She studies me for a moment before nodding. "I'm holding you to your promise."

She hurries away and I return to the dishes. Chloe excels at her position as the restaurant and bar manager for *Five Fathoms Brewing*, but she's horrible at stacking glasses for the dishwasher.

The door to the kitchen bangs open and I whirl around with a smile on my face. Chloe must really be worried about me.

The smile freezes on my face. It's not Chloe. Three people I hoped never to come across again stumble into the kitchen.

Harry, Alan, and Joe – aka the three boys who made my life living hell in junior high school. Harry and Alan are brothers and Joe is their sidekick because every group of bullies needs a sidekick.

"You shouldn't be in here." My voice wavers.

"W-w-we shouldn't be in here?" Harry pretends to stutter as he prowls toward me.

"You heard me," I force the words out and Harry stops in the middle of the kitchen a few feet from me.

Alan cackles. "We did? You barely spoke louder than a mouse."

"Holy shit!" Joe shouts. "It is a mouse. It's Mouse from junior high school."

I cringe at his use of my old nickname. I thought the nickname would be forgotten after these three moved away from Smuggler's Hideaway. But now they're back. I hope they're not back for good. They don't belong on the island. Smugglers aren't assholes. Sneaky troublemakers is more our style.

Harry crosses his arms over his chest. "Poor mouse working all alone in the kitchen and missing the party."

Alan elbows him. "She probably wants to miss the party. It's much too scary for a little mouse at such a big party."

Joe sneers. "The little mouse doesn't have a defender anymore."

I wish Caleb was here now. He'd wipe the floor with these idiots.

"Who would defend her?" Harry asks. "She's just a mouse."

"Who could love a mouse?" Alan adds.

I flinch. His words hit much too close to home. It's hard to feel loveable when the people who should love you unconditionally label you a traitor and refuse to have anything to do with you.

"Ah, look at her. She's cowering in the corner. Poor little mouse." Harry sticks out his bottom lip in a fake pout.

"You need to leave." My words are barely above a whisper but I said them. "This area is for personnel."

"Personnel?" Harry snorts. "The mouse who thought she was too good for us in junior high school is a dishwasher."

I'm not a dishwasher but I don't care to correct his assumption. It doesn't matter what he thinks. He doesn't matter.

"You need to leave," I repeat a bit louder.

Joe pulls on Harry's sleeve. "Let's go. This is boring."

"Yeah," Alan says. "There's nothing to see here."

Harry nods in agreement. "Just a little, unlovable mouse."

They stroll toward the door. Joe and Alan walk away without a backward glance, but Harry turns around to wave. "Bye, little mouse. Have a nice life living all alone on this stupid island."

I watch as the door closes behind them. I wait a few seconds before allowing the tension in my body to release.

I'm glad those assholes left the island after graduating from high school. They don't embody the feel of a smuggler.

But were they correct? A little voice asks. *Am I unlovable?*

All my insecurities come roaring back to life. Insecurities I thought I'd left behind after I moved out of my parents' house. I'm not a nobody. I finished college. I founded a brewery. I helped make the brewery a success.

All true. But what about love?

Chapter 13

"How hard can it be to cook dinner? I can stare down insurgents." ~ Caleb's famous last words

CALEB

The smoke alarm goes off and I swear. What's wrong now?

I scan the kitchen. The counter is a mess of vegetables, dishes, and knives. On the stove are two pots. The tomato sauce from one pot has erupted over the side but there's no smoke. It can't be the cause of the alarm.

Shit. There's smoke coming out of the oven. I open it and smoke blasts me. I wave a hand in front of my face as I cough.

I grab a towel and remove the smoking garlic bread. I dump it in the sink and pour water over it to stop it from smoking. The loaf has blackened, burnt edges and now it's soggy, too.

Spaghetti with garlic bread is supposed to be an easy dinner to make. My mom claimed an idiot can make it. I guess I'm worse than an idiot because the entire meal is ruined. Except the salad.

My nose wrinkles. Although I don't think the dressing turned out right since it's all clumpy.

I can't feed this to Maya. With my luck, I'll poison her and we'll end up at the hospital where everyone will laugh and point fingers at me. I shiver. The idea of being in public again after my panic attack at the restaurant makes it difficult to catch my breath.

I push down the panic. I'm in my cabin. Alone. No one's here to attack me. Once I can breathe again, I switch off the stove and oven before digging out my phone.

"Hey," Hudson answers the phone on the first ring. "What's up?"

I hear a baby cry in the background. Shit. I totally forgot Nova gave birth.

"Sorry. I shouldn't be bothering you."

"Bullshit. What do you need?"

"I ruined dinner. Any chance I can order from your restaurant and have it delivered here?"

"Is this for your dinner with Maya?"

I scowl. "She told you?"

"No. She told Nova. And before you get your panties in a twist about it, you should know Nova begged her. She even promised Maya could be the first person to babysit Iliana."

Damn. I can't complain now. I know how much Maya loves babies. She used to babysit all the time in high school. I'm surprised she hasn't had a baby of her own yet. I growl at the thought of her having a baby with anyone other than me.

"What do you want to eat?" Hudson asks. "The restaurant can make anything you want."

I check the time. Maya will be here in less than an hour. "I don't care what it is as long as it's here before Maya arrives."

"Steak and potatoes it is. I'll have the restaurant deliver it to the cabin in forty-five minutes."

"Thanks, man. I owe you."

"I'll add the cost to your monthly rent," he says and rings off.

I throw the phone on the kitchen table. I need to get this mess cleaned up before Maya gets here. I'm carrying the garbage outside when a golf cart arrives in front of the cabin. The man hands me a large bag. I sniff. The steak smells delicious.

"If you put it in the oven on low heat, it'll stay nice and warm," the man says before driving away.

I carry the food to the kitchen but hesitate to put it in the oven. The garlic bread didn't fair too well in there.

Light flashes against the kitchen window. No time to warm anything up now. I remove the food from the bags and put everything on our plates. I barely have time to throw the restaurant bags away before there's a knock on the door.

I scan the kitchen to make sure there's no evidence of my earlier attempt at cooking dinner before opening the door. Maya smiles up at me.

"Hi, Caleb."

"Hi, Bunny."

Her whiskey-colored eyes warm at my use of the nickname. Those eyes reel me in. I want to watch them heat up when I touch her skin, when I strip her clothes off of her, when I sink into her warm heat.

My cock hardens and lengthens at the vision of Maya naked and laid out on the bed for me. Her honey-blonde hair sprawled across my pillow.

I grit my teeth and wrangle my libido under control. Since I now know my bunny can handle my panic attacks, I can't help but wonder if she can handle me the man and all the dirty things I want to do to her in bed.

Maya giggles. "Are you going to invite me in?"

Damn. How long have I been standing here staring at her? It's cold outside. I usher her inside.

"Let me take your coat."

She shrugs out of her coat and I bite back a moan. She's wearing a red sweater that shows off her perky breasts and a pair of jeans that hug her curves. She looks more delicious than the food.

"What smells so good?" She walks over to the kitchen table. "Mmm... steak and potatoes."

"I hope my food choice is okay."

She rubs her hands together. "You won't hear me complaining. My hips, on the other hand, they'll hate me tomorrow."

"Your hips? Why would your hips hate you?"

She rolls her eyes. "Duh. Because they're too big and I'm not helping to make them smaller by eating this."

My gaze drops to her hips in those jeans. I want to dig my fingers into the soft flesh. "I think your hips are perfect."

"You're sweet. But there's no need to lie."

"No one's ever accused me of being sweet before." I prowl toward her and her eyes flare. My cock twitches in response but I stop before I invade her personal space.

"Liar. Ms. Simmons in kindergarten said you were a sweet boy when you helped pick up the crayons."

I snort. "Since you had to dig all the way back to kindergarten to find an example, I think you proved my point."

"I have more examples. I thought it was sweet when you called my bullies limp dicks who would never have girlfriends."

"Eighth grade. Also, a long ass time ago."

She motions to the table. "You made me dinner. Also, sweet."

I want to tell her I didn't cook. But how can I? She thinks I'm sweet. She's wrong. But it warms my chest, nonetheless.

"Shall we eat?"

She glances around the room. "Is there anything I can do?"

"Sit your sweet ass down and let me feed you."

"If you're not sweet, my ass isn't sweet."

Oh, her ass is definitely sweet. But I don't tell her as much. Maya can handle my panic attacks but I'm still not certain I'm the man for her. I left the island to prove I could be the man she needs but all I proved is I'm a screw-up who doesn't deserve friends.

I shove those memories away. I'm not spoiling my time with Maya with ghosts of the past.

"Sit," I order. "What do you want to drink? I have wine."

I didn't think of buying wine but Hudson included a bottle of red with the food.

"I brought beer."

She moves toward the bag she left at the door but I stop her with a hand in the air. "I got it."

I pour us each a beer before joining her at the table. She lifts her glass in the air.

"To friends."

I bite my tongue to stop myself from confessing how crappy a friend I can be – I don't plan for her to ever find out how I messed up my friend in the worst way – and nod.

She clinks her glass to mine before digging into her steak.

"How did you prepare the steak? Did you do some kind of rub?"

Rub? What the hell is she talking about?

"Um, yeah."

"Did you grill them outside? Or in the oven?"

She moans as she chews on her bite and my cock perks up. It wants to hear her moan when she's naked and in my bed. Skip dinner and go straight to the bedroom.

I adjust myself before cutting myself a piece of meat. "This is good."

Maya giggles. "You sound surprised. Didn't you try a piece while you were cooking?"

"No."

She unwraps her baked potato. "Wow. This is utter perfection. I love it when the outside is nice and crisp. How did you manage it without burning the skin?"

"Um…"

She leans down and sniffs the potato. "It smells as if you used some kind of herbs. What did you use?"

"Um…"

She bursts into laughter. "Your face." She points at me. She doubles over laughing until she's snorting. It shouldn't be attractive but her happiness makes my chest warm.

I cross my arms over my chest and feign annoyance. "What's funny?"

She wipes tears of laughter from her eyes and gulps in air before she calms down enough to answer.

"You pretending you made this food. With every question I asked, you got more and more flustered."

"Pretending?"

She waves a hand in the air. "You can stop. I saw the golf cart driving away from the cabin. I waited on the road for a few minutes to give you a chance to set up."

"You're sneaky."

"Hello." She taps her chest. "I'm a smuggler. It's in my blood."

"I did try to make dinner myself."

She giggles. "When you offered to cook for me, I did wonder if you'd somehow learned to cook in the past decade while you were away."

I shrug. "Why learn to cook when you can eat at the mess hall?"

She shoves a piece of steak in her mouth. "I bet the food in the mess hall wasn't as good as this."

I pick up my fork and knife. "I won't argue with you there."

"You shouldn't argue with me ever. I'm always right."

She winks at me and my heart pounds in my chest. Maya has me wrapped around her little finger and she doesn't even realize it.

I'm not the man for her but I sure as hell wish I was.

Chapter 14

"Is it wrong to ask Sammy the seal to throw my phone in the ocean?" ~ Maya

MAYA

Caleb shoves his plate away and leans back in his chair. "I'm stuffed."

"Too stuffed for the dessert I brought from *Pirates Pastries?*"

He perks up. "What did you bring?"

"A selection of cookies." I point to my bag. "You get the cookies. I'll do the dishes."

He frowns. "You're my guest. You don't have to clean."

"You cooked. I clean. Those are the rules. I didn't make them up."

"We both know I didn't cook."

I gather the dishes and pile them together. "You tried and you set the table. Good enough. Now, stop arguing and get the cookies."

I notice his limp is worse than normal when he walks to the bag, but I don't remark on it. He already knows he's limping and bringing it up will not make him a happy camper. I prefer it when he's a happy camper.

"Shall I make some coffee?"

He scowls at me. "I'll make it."

Is he annoyed I'm making myself at home? I'm not trying to invade his space. This is what friends do. When one friend isn't experimenting with living as a hermit.

Does he regret inviting me? Does he wish he could have his space to himself? Am I overthinking this? Probably.

I find the mugs and hand them to him. His earthy scent surrounds me and I barely stop myself from inhaling his scent into my lungs. I love how he smells. I wish my bed sheets smelled of him.

And now I'm perving on my friend. Knock it off, Maya. Caleb is a friend. Nothing more.

My stomach cramps – *nothing more than a friend* – but I ignore it. I should be used to ignoring my desire for more with Caleb by now.

I retreat to the sofa in the living room with the plate of cookies. Caleb joins me with coffee a few minutes later.

His eyes light up at the plate of cookies. "I haven't had a cookie from *Pirates Pastries* forever."

"Go ahead. They're fresh. Parker was pulling them out of the oven when I arrived."

"Parker?" He raises an eyebrow. "The girl who was a class behind us in high school?"

"The one and the same. She owns the bakery now."

He bites into a cookie and moans. "Damn. Parker can bake."

"Which is probably why she owns a bakery."

He chuckles. "You are—"

My phone rings and cuts him off. I dig it out of my purse but frown when I notice the number. Why is she phoning me?

I stand. "I need to take this."

I glance around the cabin but there's nowhere I can go for privacy. Unless I want to stand in the bathroom – ew. Or outside – too cold. Or Caleb's bedroom – too much temptation. I end up sitting at the kitchen table.

"Hello."

"It's about time you answered," Mom snipes.

Exaggerate much? The phone rang three times.

"Hi, Mom. What's happening?" I haven't spoken to my mom in years. It's hard to have a relationship with someone when they kick you out of the house on your eighteenth birthday.

"What's happening is I want you to stop making a fool of yourself."

A fool of myself? I haven't made a fool out of myself.

"What are you talking about?"

"You," she sneers. "Galivanting around the island with Caleb. A man who will never love you."

Those words hit their mark but I don't let on. She'd enjoy pouring salt on the wound and rubbing it in if she realized she injured me.

I snort instead. "I haven't galivanted anywhere."

"Don't lie to me," she hisses. "Everyone on the island knows you went to dinner with his family at *Smuggler's Cove*."

"Dinner and galivanting aren't the same thing."

"You always think you're so much smarter than everyone else. Where has being the smart girl gotten you? Huh?"

I don't bother answering. She's on a rant and won't hear me anyway. Trust me. I've had enough experience with her rants.

"You're living on Smuggler's Hideaway all by yourself. You'll always be all by yourself. Who the hell could ever love you?"

She stops ranting and I wait for her to continue. When she doesn't, I ask, "Are you finished?"

"Stop making a fool of yourself. You're embarrassing me and your father."

She hangs up before I can explain how I'm not embarrassing anyone. How is having dinner with Caleb and his family embarrassing to her? What does she think I did – fawn all over Caleb?

I throw my phone on the table and rub a hand over my forehead where I feel a headache coming on.

"Who was on the phone?" Caleb asks from right next to me and I startle. I forgot I wasn't alone. Great. Now, I'm the one who's embarrassed.

"No one."

"No one?" He raises an eyebrow. "It didn't sound like no one."

It's stupid to lie when he could hear the conversation. Or, at least, my part of the conversation. "Fine. It was my mom."

His brow wrinkles. "I thought you didn't have contact with her."

"She rings every decade or so to remind me how unlovable I am."

"Unlovable?" He growls. "You're not unlovable."

"Mom thinks otherwise," I say instead of admitting how true her words feel to me. How else should I feel when the people who are supposed to love me unconditionally don't?

"It's their loss. It has nothing to do with you."

"Oh yeah? It felt as if it had something to do with me when they kicked me out of the house on my eighteenth birthday and told me never to come back."

"They kicked you out? Why didn't you ever tell me?"

"You were off at basic training. What were you supposed to do?"

"You could have told me afterwards."

Admit I'm unlovable to the man I've wanted since second grade? I don't think so. I wave a hand in dismissal. "Forget about it. It's over and done with."

"Doesn't seem to be over and done with. You're obviously upset."

As much as I wish I could claim I'm not upset, I can't. I still long for my parents to love me. They're my parents. They're supposed to love me. But they don't. They consider me a traitor. Because sticking up for what you believe in makes you a traitor.

"Can we move on? I don't want to talk about my parents."

"Admit you're upset and I'll drop it."

I fist my hands on my hips. "Are you serious? You'll drop it if I say what you want me to say? What kind of bullshit is this? I don't push you on your issues."

"You showed up here three times and demanded entrance despite me telling you I wanted to be left alone."

"And you didn't let me in, so I dropped it."

He snorts. "You didn't drop it. My parents showed up and thought we were a couple."

I shrug. "We can stop pretending to date whenever you want. I'm helping you out."

"Help me out now and admit you're upset."

I huff. "You're worse than a dog with a bone."

He chuckles. "You have no idea how much worse I can get. Say what I want to hear."

"No. I'm not saying shit. I'm out of here."

I stomp toward the door but Caleb shackles my wrist and whirls me around to face him. "I'm serious, Maya. If you don't admit how your parents upset you, they'll continue to have power over you."

"What are you? Some psychiatrist now?"

"Nope. I'm a man who watched his girlfriend become devastated by whatever her mom said to her."

"Fake girlfriend," I remind him.

"Whatever. You're my friend. I hate to see you hurt."

"Then, let me go and you won't see it anymore."

"I'll still be aware of how upset you are."

I stomp my foot. "I'm warning you, Caleb. Let this go."

He leans close until he's right in my face. "Or what, Maya? What are you going to do?"

"I'll… I'll…"

I do the only thing I can think of. I push up on my toes and mold my lips to his. Blackbeard's tale. This was a bad idea. I didn't need to know how Caleb tastes. His flavor is as complex as a storm – salty, electric, and utterly consuming.

He licks my bottom lip and I moan.

"Let me in, Maya," he grumbles.

I can't resist his plea. I don't want to. I open and he plunges his tongue into my mouth. He plunders my mouth as if he can't get enough of me. As if he savors every inch of my mouth. As if I'm the only woman in the world.

He shoves his hard cock against my belly and I gasp before grabbing hold of his shoulders.

I should probably stop him. I should probably run away before he breaks my heart.

But I'm no fool. If this is my only chance to taste and touch and feel the man, I've been obsessed with for over a decade, I'm not going anywhere.

I'm holding on for the ride.

Chapter 15

"There's only so much temptation a man can take." ~ *Caleb*

CALEB

I should stop. Maya deserves better than me. She deserves a better man.

Except the 'man' who told me she deserved better kicked her out of his house when she was eighteen. I knew Maya's relationship with her parents was bad. But I didn't question her. She avoided the subject and I let her.

I screwed up. I should have pressured her. I've been away for years – away from Maya for years – for nothing.

Maya's taste of honey fills me and I forget all about the past and the mistakes I've made. All I can think of now is my desire for her. A desire I've kept leashed for thirteen years. A desire born after our one kiss.

I drag my lips away from hers and pepper kisses along her jaw until I reach her ear.

"Do you want to stop?"

"No," she breathes out.

"Are you sure?"

She nods.

I bite her earlobe. "There's no going back from this."

"If you're going to talk the entire time, I want dirty talk."

"My shy girl wants dirty talk, she'll get dirty talk."

Her body shivers against mine. "Oh goodie."

I chuckle. My bunny never ceases to amuse me.

"Wrap your legs around me." She doesn't hesitate. Once her legs are around my waist, I carry her to the bedroom.

"No wall sex?" Maya pouts.

I nip her bottom lip. "I want you in my bed where I can lay you out and sample you like a buffet."

Her legs tighten around me. "I approve."

I lay her down on the bed and come down on top of her. "I want to strip you bare."

Her breath hitches. "I'm not stopping you."

I kneel between her legs and my thigh protests. I ignore it. My injury is not going to ruin my first time with Maya. I refuse to let it.

"Arms up."

Her whiskey eyes stare directly into mine as she slowly lifts her arms. My shy girl is a temptress in bed. Duly noted. And appreciated.

She bats her eyelashes. "Now what?"

I grasp the edge of her sweater. "Now I unwrap my present."

I draw the material up her body, making sure to skim her sides as I go. Goosebumps follow in my wake. I love how responsive she is to me.

I whip the sweater off of her and throw it behind me, leaving Maya in a pink bra and a turquoise bracelet.

I tap the bracelet. "Is this...?"

She smiles. "Yes. I always wear it. I never take it off."

She wears the bracelet I bought her for her twenty-first birthday nearly a decade ago? More proof I'm a fucking idiot when it comes to Maya. No more. I'm done denying myself.

Starting now. My gaze returns to her pretty pink bra. I trace the lacy edge with my index finger.

"Such a pretty bra. Does the pink match the color of your nipples?"

Her cheeks darken at my question but she doesn't duck her chin to hide from me. "There's one way to find out."

"I do love a challenge."

I flick the bra open and the material falls out of my way. I want to admire her bare breasts, but I can't resist touching. I knead and mold the mounds until her nipples form hard points.

"Caleb," she moans.

"What do you need, Bunny?"

"You. To touch me."

"Am I not touching you now?"

"Not where I need it," she pouts.

"You mean this?" I pinch her nipple and she moans. "Or this?" I lean forward and take her breast into my mouth. She writhes beneath me.

"Yes."

She threads her hands through my hair and shoves my face closer to her chest. And here I was worried my Maya would be shy in bed.

My cock presses against my zipper and urges me to move things along. I release her nipple and kiss my way down her chest. I reach her jeans and don't waste any time in unzipping them and shoving them down her legs.

"Shit," I mutter when I realize she's still wearing her boots.

Maya gets up on her elbows. "This never happens in romance novels."

"Do their boots magically disappear?"

She shrugs. Her breasts bounce with the movement and my cock twitches. I need to get a move on before I come in my pants like a freaking teenager.

I unzip Maya's boots and pull them off. Next, I remove her jeans and socks. She's completely naked to me now except for a pair of pink panties.

She grasps the edge of the panties and begins to shove them down her legs. I stop her.

"Nuh-uh. I get to remove your clothes."

"You were taking too long."

"It's not my fault your boots didn't magically disappear like in a romance novel."

She giggles and the sound hits me in the chest. It spreads warmth through areas of me I didn't think would ever feel warm again.

Maya doesn't know it yet, but things have changed. I'm not letting her go. I'm done holding myself back from her.

But first. I'm going to make her come so many times she'll never want to leave this bed.

I draw her panties down her legs before tapping her thigh. "Widen your legs for me."

Her lack of hesitation has my cock pulsing. I inhale a deep breath to get myself under control before I lay on the bed in between her legs. I draw my hands up her thighs. Her skin is smooth and unblemished by any scars.

I draw my nose along her lips and inhale her honey scent. I'm fucking addicted to the scent. I pull her lips apart to expose her clit.

I draw circles around it with my tongue and Maya digs her nails into my head. "More."

"You want me to make you come with my tongue?"

"Yes," she hisses.

I lick and suck until I figure out what makes Maya squirm. And then I settle in to drive her absolutely mad. I want her riding my face. I want her juices leaking out of her. I want her crazy with desire.

When she wraps her legs around my neck, I smile. I tease her opening with my finger. I inch in and out. Just enough to drive her nuts.

"Caleb," she growls. "Stop teasing me."

My cock agrees. It's done with the teasing. It wants to feel Maya's wet warmth surrounding it. It wants to bury itself inside Maya until I don't know where she ends and I begin.

I feel a tingling in my lower back and mutter a swear. I am not coming in my damn jeans. Teasing time is over.

I suck on her clit and plunge two fingers into her pussy. Her walls immediately convulse around me.

"Yes, yes, yes," she chants as she rides out her orgasm.

I continue to thrust in and out of her until she collapses on the bed. I get to my knees.

"Watch me," I command her.

Her eyes fly open and I lick her juices off of my fingers. Her eyes flare.

"I never thought it was sexy when a man licked his fingers in a book before. I was wrong."

"There's something else you're wrong about."

"What?"

"When you come, you say my name."

Her eyes widen. "Are you going to make me come again?"

I smirk. "Hell, yeah, I am."

"Oh goodie."

I start to whip my shirt off before I remember. I don't want Maya to see my scars and injuries. I don't want her to pity me. It's bad enough, my thigh is trembling.

She notices my hesitation. "What's wrong?"

"I forgot to switch the light off."

She frowns. "But then I won't be able to see you."

Exactly.

She sits up. "What's the problem?"

I glance away. "My body is not a pretty sight."

She snorts and I scowl.

"Sorry." She holds up a hand. "But it's comical how you think your body isn't a pretty sight when it's actually absolutely gorgeous."

"You haven't seen the scars."

She lays her palm on my cheek. "Those scars are badges of honor. You got them defending our country. Making it a safe place for me to live. They're nothing to be ashamed of."

"I'm not a hero."

"You are to me."

I look into her eyes but I don't note any deception or pity there. She's serious. But she'll change her mind when she sees the scars on my body. I don't want to tarnish her image of me, but the image she has is wrong.

"Switch off the lights. I don't want you to be uncomfortable."

I don't hesitate. I roll off the bed and walk to the door where the light switch is.

"But Caleb," she calls and I pause, "you're still a hero."

I hit the lights before she notices my flinch. I'm not a fucking hero. I'm the furthest thing from it. I should keep my hands stained with the blood of my friend off of Maya but I won't.

I dig a condom out of my bedside drawer before undressing and joining Maya back on the bed. There's a little light from the moon outside but I can't make out Maya's facial expressions.

Damn. I want to watch her face as I sink into her. Maybe next time I'll keep my clothes on.

I crawl back on the bed. I blanket Maya with my body. She grasps my shoulders and I grit my teeth. She can't see me but if she explores my skin with her hands, she'll discover how damaged I am.

"Hands on the headboard," I order.

This time she hesitates to follow my order. But I can't let her touch my body. She'll feel the scars and have questions. The answers to which will prove I'm no hero. I want to be a hero in her eyes a bit longer.

When she removes her hands from my body, I reward her by notching my cock at her entrance. She wraps her legs around me and I sink into her. She's tight but I don't stop until my balls slap her ass.

Damn. She feels good. Better than anyone else I've ever had. Good thing I've stopped denying myself what I want because I am not letting her go.

She moans. "This is better than any sex in all the books I've read."

"Hell, yeah, it is," I grumble before retreating.

I'll show her sex with me is better than a book. I'll get her addicted to me the way I am to her.

Chapter 16

"Why is it called a walk of shame? It should be a parade of happiness." ~ Maya when she's delirious after sex

MAYA

I wake surrounded by warmth and the earthy scent of Caleb. I snuggle into him and he tightens his arm around me.

This is everything I ever wanted. Everything I ever dreamed of. Everything I never thought I'd have.

Caleb – the man I've wanted since our kiss in the library senior year of high school – is in this bed with me after making love to me all night long.

A sliver of doubt creeps in. Is this everything Caleb wants? Or was he merely letting off steam? Carried away by the moment. I did kiss him first after all.

Maybe I should go home before things get awkward.

I lift Caleb's arm and slide toward the edge of the bed. I'm nearly there when his arm clamps down on me.

"Where are you going? I'm not done with you yet."

Despite having more orgasms last night than I've had in the past year, I shiver as excitement bolts through me. I imagine all the dirty things Caleb can do to me and my panties dampen in response.

I roll around to face him. I frown when I notice he's wearing a long sleeved t-shirt and sweats. The only skin exposed is his hands and face. He's afraid I'll be repelled by any scars he has.

He doesn't understand. Those scars are pieces of him. And I love him. I wouldn't be repelled by him.

Fear snakes through my belly. *I love Caleb.* I've denied my feelings for too many years. Claimed we're friends and I didn't want more. But I can't deny my feelings any longer. Not after last night. I blew the 'we're just friends' excuse to smithereens.

Speaking of friends.

"Last night doesn't have to mean anything."

His brow furrows. "Doesn't have to mean anything?"

"We can go back to being friends."

Those words kill me to say but I don't want to lose Caleb. If friends is all he's capable of, I'll take what I can get.

"Go back to being friends?"

"Are you going to repeat everything I say this morning?"

"When you say stupid shit, yes."

I scowl. "I didn't say stupid shit."

"Saying we can go back to being friends is stupid."

Does Caleb not want to be friends anymore? My heart squeezes, and I find it difficult to catch my breath. I can't lose him.

"You don't want to be friends anymore?"

"Nope."

I grasp my chest as pain lances through it. I'm losing Caleb. I'm such an idiot. I never should have had sex with him. Sex ruins everything. I know better.

I've read thousands of romance novels. I know what happens when the couple has sex before one of them is ready to admit they want more.

Realization hits me. Caleb doesn't want more. He was scratching an itch last night.

"Stop," he growls.

Tears well in my eyes. I blink to stop them from falling but it's a lost cause. They course down my face.

Caleb wraps his arms around me. "Fuck."

I fight his hold. "Let me go."

"Bunny, I'm never letting you go."

"I need to go."

He pinches my chin and tilts my head up until our gazes clash. "Did you hear me? I'm never letting you go."

"You can't—"

I slam my mouth shut when I realize he's disagreeing with me. I wipe the tears from my cheeks. "Wait. What did you say?"

He nudges my hands out of the way to take over wiping my tears. "I'm never letting you go, Bunny."

"But we're friends. You don't want more."

"I've always wanted more."

My mouth gapes open. "You did?"

He kisses my nose. "Yes."

"But why didn't you tell me? Why did you stay away for so long?"

He glances away. "I wasn't ready."

"You weren't ready?" I snort. "Is this your way of letting me down easy? You're worried how I'm going to react so you lie and say you've always wanted me?" I shake my head. "You don't want me."

How could he? My own parents don't want me. Why would Caleb, the man who could have any woman he wants with a crook of his finger, want me?

"I'm pretty sure I showed you how much I want you last night."

"It was—"

He growls. "Don't you dare tell me it was only sex. It was more than sex and you know it."

"But—"

"No. I'm not listening to whatever bullshit you're thinking up to put me back in the friend zone. I finally got out of there and I'm not going back."

"Not going back?"

He nods. "You and me? This relationship? It's no longer fake. We're doing this."

"You've decided and that's all there is to it?"

"Yep."

I glare at him. "You can't unilaterally decide we're a couple."

"I can and I did."

"This is not how things work!"

I try to shove him away but he captures my hands. "Do you not want to be in a relationship with me?"

"I didn't say I don't want to be in a relationship with you."

"Then, why are you fighting me?"

Because I can't believe it. All my dreams are coming true. I thought my dreams coming true would be exciting. It's not. It's scary. More than scary. It's terrifying.

What happens when Caleb realizes I'm not loveable? How will I survive it when the man I love walks away from me?

It won't break my heart. It'll rip my heart clean out of my chest.

I can't chance it. I won't.

Caleb presses his lips to mine. "Don't fight me, Bunny."

I try to respond but he kisses me again.

"Don't get me wrong, I'll fight you. But I don't want to." He nibbles along my jaw. "I have more interesting things I'd rather do." He presses his hard length against my belly. "Do you want to fight or fuck?"

My whole body shivers.

Despite knowing this is a bad idea, I don't stop him when he slips a hand under my t-shirt and begins to massage my breast.

Despite knowing this is going to lead to heartache, I don't protest when he draws the shirt off of me and rolls me onto my back.

Despite knowing this is going to ruin our friendship, I don't say a word when he pulls out his cock, dons a condom, and lines it up to my opening.

"I promise you won't regret giving me – us – a chance," Caleb vows as he inches inside me. I cling to his shoulders as he sinks into me. "Because this is where I belong."

He slowly withdraws before thrusting into me again. I moan at the feeling of him filling me up. Sex with Caleb is everything I've ever dreamed about. It's even better than I imagined. And, trust me, I have quite the imagination. There's a reason I'm obsessed with romance books after all.

"Will you give me a chance?" he asks and I can't deny him.

It was hard enough to deny him before he was inside me. But now that he's filling me up and I'm surrounded by everything Caleb, I can't say no. I don't want to. I never wanted to.

"Okay," I whisper.

"Thank you, Maya. You won't regret it." He kisses my forehead before smirking. "I'm going to show you how much you won't regret it now."

He begins pounding into me and all my worries about the future disappear as I let everything Caleb overwhelm my senses and my thoughts.

Chapter 17

"For Maya, I'll do anything. Even risk another embarrassing panic attack." ~ Caleb

CALEB

Maya clings to my hand as we walk up my parent's driveway for Sunday lunch. I've avoided Sunday lunches since I've been home but I'm going to try. For her. I'll do anything for her.

I want Maya to realize she's not alone in the world. Her parents are assholes but she's got me and my family. She has her friends. She is wanted. She is loved.

"There's no reason to be nervous."

"Easy for you to say," she mutters.

I lift an eyebrow.

Her brow furrows before understanding lights her eyes and she gasps. "I'm sorry. I didn't think about how hard this would be for you. We can go back home. Not home. The cabin. I mean the cabin. Your cabin. Not mine. Not ours."

I enjoy it when she calls the cabin home. I want her to feel she has a home with me. Because she's my home. My center of gravity. The person I depend on above everyone else. The person I want at my side through all of life's trials.

She's my everything. For too long I pushed her away. Kept her firmly in the friend zone. No more.

The door flies open and my sisters – Willow, Abigail, Clara, and Eliza – crowd the entrance.

"Too late to run away now," I mutter.

"I can cover you while you flee."

She's cute. She thinks she can cover me. I kiss her nose. "I'm staying. Being around my family doesn't make me as anxious as crowds do."

It costs me to admit to the weakness but Maya's smile makes it worthwhile. "If you get panicky, give me a signal."

"Panicky? A signal?"

"Tug on your ear three times and I'll whisk you away."

I chuckle. My Maya is cute and adorable. Have I mentioned what an idiot I was for staying away from her?

"I knew it!" Willow shouts.

"Knew what?" I ask as we step onto the porch.

"You two are a couple."

My brow wrinkles. "Of course, we're a couple. We had dinner together for you to meet her."

Abigail rolls her eyes. "You were faking it. We all knew it."

"You did?" Maya asks. "How?"

Clara sighs. "I'm glad you're not faking it now. You two are adorable together."

"Can you imagine how their babies will look?" Eliza asks. "They'll be beautiful."

"B-b-babies?" Maya asks. Her grip on my hand tightens.

"Now, you've done it." Willow frowns. "You're scaring her."

"I'm sorry," Eliza says. "I didn't mean to scare you."

"I'm not scared," Maya claims.

Abigail points to my hand. "Which is why big brother no longer has any blood circulating in his hand."

Maya glances down at our hands. When she notices mine is white, she releases it and steps back. "I'm sorry. I didn't mean…"

I wrap an arm around her. "You can't hurt me, Maya."

She narrows her eyes at me. "Are you saying I'm a wimp? I'll have you know I took self-defense classes in college."

I kiss her hair. "I've officially been warned, Bunny."

Clara claps. "He calls her bunny."

"I warned you my sisters are troublemakers."

Maya giggles. "I can handle troublemakers. Have you met my friends?"

"Come inside and shut the door! There's no need to warm the outside," Dad yells and Maya jumps.

I frown down at her. "Are you sure you're okay? We can go back home."

"I'm okay." Her wide eyes and soft voice contradict her words but I don't get a chance to question her further before Mom arrives.

"Come in. Come in." Mom herds everyone inside. "What's this I hear about the two of you being a couple?"

"Mom," I grumble. "You knew we were a couple already."

She dismisses my words with a flick of her wrist. "Everyone knows you were faking."

I scan the room. "How does everyone know?"

"Never mind," Mom says. "Now we can properly welcome Maya to the family."

Maya's eyes widen and she shuffles until she's standing slightly behind me. Mom isn't having it. She grasps Maya's hands and pulls her into a hug.

"Welcome to the family, Maya!"

"Mom," I warn.

"What? I'm being warm and welcoming. This is what a mother does when her son who never visits home finally settles down."

"I'm not..." I trail off when I hear Maya sniffle.

"You better not have made Maya cry." I pull Maya away from Mom and scowl at the tears on her face.

"Oh dear," Mom mutters. "I didn't mean to make you cry."

"It's okay," Maya says but the tears continue to course down her face. "They're happy tears."

I shackle her wrist and lead her down the hallway to the bathroom. I shut and lock the door behind us before lifting Maya onto the vanity.

I frame her face with my hands. "What's wrong, Bunny? Do you want to leave?"

"I don't want to leave. These are happy tears." She smiles up at me but her bottom lip trembles.

I growl. "I don't want you to cry. I don't care if the tears are happy tears."

She slaps my chest. "Get used to it, soldier. I'll cry if I want to."

I groan. "I've created a monster."

"Are you saying I'm a monster? Do I get to wear green paint and have horns? Are you a monster, too? Do you have a tail?"

"What are they talking about?" Willow shouts.

"Shush. I can't hear them," Clara claims.

"They're talking about monsters," Abigail says.

"Oh, I've read about this. It's called monster romance," Eliza says.

I lean my forehead against Maya's. "Welcome to the madhouse."

"I think it's wonderful. I always wanted sisters or brothers. Being an only child is boring especially when…"

I pinch her chin. "Especially when what?"

She forces a smile. "Never mind. Shall we get back out there? Your sisters will think we're having sex in here if we linger any longer."

"No, we won't," Eliza shouts.

"But we will listen in," Willow adds.

"Did I say I wanted sisters?" Maya mumbles. "I think I was wrong."

The door flies open and my sisters hurry inside.

"We're the best sisters," Abigail claims.

"I don't think sisters are supposed to barge into the bathroom when the door is locked," Maya mutters.

Willow snorts. "You don't understand how sisters work."

Clara grabs my wrist and pulls Maya away from me. "Come on. Mom got Caleb's baby books out."

Maya perks up and allows Clara to lead her away. "Baby books?"

"Maya," I call. She glances at me over her shoulder and I pull on my earlobe three times.

"Are you afraid of me looking at your baby books?"

I puff out my chest. "Of course not. I was a beautiful baby."

"But you gave the signal."

"I was teasing you." I wink.

"You're okay?"

Her cheeks are stained from her tears but she's worried about me. Warmth hits my chest. This woman is everything.

"I'm okay. Go." I shoo her away. "Have fun."

"Awesome," Willow declares and my sisters herd Maya down the hallway to the living room. I follow. I scowl when I realize Clara wasn't joking. Mom did get out the baby books.

Dad hands me a beer. "Let's go watch the game in the basement."

"What game?"

My dad has never been into sports much. He'd rather be outside fishing or hunting or working on some project.

He shrugs. "No idea but there must be some game on."

I catch Maya's eye. *You okay?* I mouth.

She winks and pulls on her earlobe twice.

"Look at this one," Abigail declares.

"Ah, little Caleb is in the bath."

"Not the bath photo." Abigail taps the page. "This one."

Maya bursts into laughter. "Is Caleb wearing a pumpkin outfit?"

Mom joins Maya on the sofa. "He wouldn't take it off for an entire week. Do you know how awful a baby stinks if he isn't washed for a week?" She pinches her nose.

"Maybe a hockey game is on," I mutter to Dad who chuckles as we descend the stairs to the basement.

I'm grumbling but I don't care. If Maya wants to go through all of my baby pictures, she can have at it. As long as it makes her happy and she feels comfortable with my family, I'm happy.

Because Maya deserves a family of her own. She deserves everything.

And I'm going to do my best to give it to her.

Chapter 18

"I'm going to stop going to the grocery store. Maybe I'll start Smuggler's Hideaway's first grocery delivery service." ~ Maya

MAYA

I message Caleb as I hurry into the grocery store.

Do you need anything from the store?

I can do my own groceries.

I roll my eyes. I know he can do his own groceries. I'm trying to be helpful here. But sometimes Mr. Protector takes his role a little too seriously.

I'm at the store now.

Three dots appear and disappear several times. I grab a cart in the meantime.

Oh okay. Can you grab some bread and milk? Please.

On it. Be there in thirty minutes.

I type *Love You* but stop myself before I hit send. Phew. Caleb and I haven't been a couple very long. I don't plan on throwing out 'love yous' until we're more secure in our relationship. In other words, I'm not going to be the first to drop the three-word bomb.

It almost never ends well in a romance novel when the woman confesses her love first. It's better if the man bares his heart before she does. And since I'm not planning to get my heart broken by Caleb, I'll keep my love bombs to myself.

"Hey, Maya," Hazel greets from the other side of the produce department.

I wave at her.

"How's Caleb?" She waggles her eyebrows.

I glance around to ensure no one else is listening to us. There are a few customers who appear a bit too interested in their oranges so I steer my cart closer to Hazel.

"Keep your voice down," I hiss at her.

"Your relationship with Caleb isn't a secret. You came to the restaurant together."

I feel my cheeks heat at her challenging tone, but I force my legs to stay planted and not run away.

"Caleb is a very private person. I don't need to remind you of how private he is, do I?"

"Fine," she gives in. "I won't pester you with questions about how good Caleb is in bed. Considering you spent most of high school in detention, I thought you were more fun."

She marches off and the tension in my shoulders relaxes. Crisis averted.

I hurry through the store while filling my cart with everything on my list. I'm anxious to see Caleb again. I was busy working on the quarterly accounts yesterday and didn't make it out to the cabin last night.

It's only been four days since we removed the 'fake' from our relationship but I want to spend all my time with Caleb. I want to make up for all the years we missed.

I round the corner into the final aisle to get some bread for Caleb and I nearly crash into a woman. Not just any woman. My mother.

I can't believe this. I haven't had contact with my family – except to send Christmas and birthday cards – for years. But this is the second time I've had contact with Mom this month. Is there a blue moon or something?

I decide to ignore her. She's done it to me for years. How hard can it be?

I steer my cart around her but she latches onto it and uses it to block me from leaving.

"Trying to avoid your mother?" Mom sneers.

"Um…" I bite my lip as I try to come up with a lie. Mom hates to be ignored. Never mind how she's ignored me for years.

"Um. Ah. Still the same old shy girl who can't stand up for herself?"

I stood up for Mom once – it was one of the most difficult things I've done in my life – and look where it got me. Kicked out of the house at eighteen and ignored for more than a decade.

"Hi, Mom."

I hate calling this woman my mother. She was never a mother to me. She never shielded me from Dad's rage. She never nurtured or cared for me. She was too busy catering to all Dad's needs and wants. Fat lot of good it did her.

"Hi, Mom," she mimics.

Wonderful. We've reached the 'making fun of Maya' portion of the evening. And here I was worried there wouldn't be time for it.

"I need to..." I trail off when I notice the man making his way down the aisle. My hands tighten on the cart until my fingernails dig into my palms.

"Roger," Mom hollers to my dad. "Guess who I ran into?"

Dad glowers at Mom before glancing my way. His eyes are the same shade of brown as mine but they're devoid of any emotion. With those flat eyes, it's a mystery to me how the inhabitants of Smuggler's Island don't recognize Dad for what he is – a monster.

"What are you doing here?" Dad asks.

I want to snark at him. Ask him what he thinks I'm doing at a grocery store. But those empty eyes hold me entranced and words won't form.

"Um..."

Mom snorts. "For the life of me, I can't understand why you think you're so much better than us. You can't even form words or speak properly."

I do not think I'm better than them. I'm just me. I'm not better or worse than any other person. But Mom is convinced I think I'm better than her because I refuse to accept Dad's abuse.

Standing up for myself is not the same as thinking I'm better than anyone.

"I don't think I'm better than you."

"What did you say?" Mom shouts her question. "I couldn't hear you over the sound of the background music."

Dad chuckles. "Maya always was a little scared mouse."

I am not a mouse. Was I scared in his house? Hell, yeah, I was. Any child would have been.

Even Mom was scared. She won't admit it, but her eyes were filled with fright every time Dad came home from work. But when she was offered an out, she didn't take it. For some reason, it's all my fault. Dad's abuse. Her refusal to leave. All of it. My fault.

I notice people have stopped shopping to watch our interaction. My face warms even further under their scrutiny.

"I… ah… should be…" I try to wheel my cart away but Mom won't release her hold on it. I wiggle the cart but she doesn't budge. I could probably break away. But I'm not hurting her. That's my dad's job.

"But we haven't had a chance to catch up yet." She tries to make her voice sound sweet but it reminds me of nails on a chalkboard.

I grit my teeth. "Catch up?"

Mom and Dad haven't talked to me in years and now they want to catch up? What's going on? Why are they torturing me? Why would—

I'm such an idiot. The answer is obvious. They want to bring me down a peg.

They usually let me live my life. But now that I have something – someone – to lose they're using this opportunity to try and ruin my happiness.

They always ruin my happiness. When I came home from school excited about my good grades or winning a spelling bee or getting the top grade on a math test, they'd set in on me. Tease me or torture me with nasty words until I learned to keep things to myself.

"I want to hear all about how the plain mouse managed to snag the hottest man on Smuggler's Hideaway," Mom says.

Dad laughs. "They must be faking it. Caleb would never dare to date Maya."

We were faking it. But we're not anymore. I want to open my mouth and scream at him. Tell him he's wrong. But one look at the muscle pulsing in his jaw and the words get stuck in my throat. I know what his look means. It's not good.

"She could never make him happy. Who can love a plain mouse?"

I nearly flinch at those words. How can anyone love me? My own parents don't love me. And they're supposed to love me unconditionally. But they'd rather tear me down than build me up and have me be happy. They want me to join them in their misery.

"Nothing to say for yourself, little mouse?" Mom teases.

I have a lot to say but I know better than to open my mouth. It's a waste of time and energy. They won't listen to me anyway.

"Let's go, Geraldine." Dad wraps a hand around Mom's bicep and drags her away. She winces and I know he's hurting her. He's always hurting her. But she won't leave him.

I watch as Dad yanks Mom down the aisle. When they turn the corner, I follow on my tiptoes to make sure they're actually leaving.

I hide behind a cereal display and watch them walk out the exit. Mom is practically running to keep up with Dad's long strides but he doesn't slow down for her. He doesn't take anyone into consideration except himself. Selfish prick.

My phone buzzes in my pocket and I pull it out. *Caleb calling.*

Did the smuggler grapevine tell him what happened? Does he know what a wimp I am? How I become mute whenever my parents confront me?

I drop the phone back into my pocket. I can't deal with him now. I don't want him to realize how unlovable I truly am.

I abandon my cart where it is and rush out of the grocery store. I aim for the one place I know I'm safe. A place my parents would never dare step foot in.

I'll hide there while I figure out what to do.

Should I break up with Caleb before he has the chance to break my heart?

Or should I enjoy him while I can? Until he realizes I'm unlovable?

Chapter 19

"This is not the time for a fucking test." ~ Caleb

CALEB

I frown when my call to Maya goes to voicemail. She always answers her phone. Even when she's in line to check out at the grocery store or in a meeting with clients. She always answers me.

Maybe she's driving and forgot to plug in her Bluetooth? I check the clock. I'll give her fifteen minutes and then I'll try again.

Fourteen minutes later I'm pacing the cabin and wondering what's wrong. I've called Maya's phone three more times and all my calls have gone to voicemail.

I dial Hudson.

"Hey man," he answers.

"Can I speak to Nova?"

"What's wrong?"

"I can't reach Maya. She was going to stop by the grocery store before coming to my place but it's been more than an hour since she messaged me."

"Hold on. Nova is trying Maya now."

I scowl. "Why would Maya answer Nova's call but not mine?"

"Who knows why women do what they do? But it's worth checking. Hold on. Nova wants to speak to you."

"What did you do?" Nova asks.

I rear back at the angry tone of her voice. "What did I do?"

"Yes. What did you do? Maya's not answering my call either."

"Shit." I rub a hand down my face. "I have a bad feeling."

"What did you do? Don't make me come over there. Or send Hudson over there to kick your ass."

"I didn't do anything. She was stopping at the grocery store on her way here. I asked her to pick up bread and milk."

She blows out a breath. "Okay. Here's Hudson."

"I'll message you Flynn and Lucas's numbers."

"What? I need to find Maya. Not make friends."

"Flynn is engaged to Sophia, and Lucas is married to Chloe."

"Oh." Sophia and Chloe are two of Maya's posse. Maya has told me all about their love lives in her letters but in my need to get to Maya, I forgot.

He hangs up and my phone beeps with a message seconds later.

I dial Flynn first. From what I remember in high school, Sophia was more levelheaded than Chloe.

"Here's Sophia," Flynn says instead of greeting me.

"What did you do?" Sophia asks.

I'm about done with being accused of hurting Maya. I would never hurt her. I love her.

I love her.

I've been fighting my feelings for her for far too long but I'm done fighting. Maya is everything I need. She fills up the cold corners of my soul. She calms me when I feel as if I'm going out of my skin. She drives me crazy with desire.

She's it. She's my person.

"I didn't do anything," I grit out. "I need to find Maya. She could be hurt and all you care about is gossip."

She sighs. "About time you stopped hesitating."

"Were you fucking testing me?"

"Hell yeah, I was. Maya is fragile. I don't want her hurt."

"You don't know Maya at all. She isn't fragile. She's a warrior."

A fragile woman doesn't handle a man having a panic attack the way she did. Maya's shy but she's not soft.

Sophia squeals. "I love this! Maya is finally getting her happy ever after."

I grunt. "Can we discuss our relationship later?" As in never. "I need to find Maya now."

"Remember you promised to discuss your relationship later," Sophia says.

"Maya. Where is Maya?"

"I don't know. She apparently had a confrontation with her parents at the grocery store."

I growl. "What? What the hell happened? Did they hurt her?"

"I wasn't there, but rumor has it her parents humiliated her in the cereal aisle."

"I'm going to kill them."

"You probably shouldn't make threats to kill people on an unsecure line."

She doesn't need to worry. If I want to eliminate Maya's parents, no one will know what happened to them. It's hard to prosecute a person for murder when there are no bodies.

"Where's Maya now?" I need to get to her. She's probably upset. Her parents are assholes to her. I need to comfort her. I don't want her going through this alone.

"She's not at home. Chloe checked there already."

I grab my keys and rush out of the cabin. "Where else could she be? Where should I search?"

"The brewery is the only place I can think of."

I switch on my truck. "I'm on my way there."

"I'll let Chloe know."

Before I have the chance to ask why, she hangs up.

I pay no attention to the rough driveway. I bounce up and down as I speed toward the main road. I grit my teeth as pain shoots from my foot through my leg to my groin, but I don't slow down.

I make it to the main road and hit the gas. I'm speeding and should probably be on the lookout for Sammy the seal but I can't be bothered. I need to find Maya. She's hurting and all alone.

My phone rings and I hit answer on my dashboard.

"Why didn't you contact me?" Paisley asks.

"What?"

"I'm Maya's friend, too."

Good point. Paisley is the smartest of the group. I should have phoned her first.

"I didn't have your number."

"You do now. I'm sending you Maya's location."

"You know where Maya is?"

"Of course, I do. This is why you should have phoned me first."

She hangs up but my phone beeps with a notification seconds later. I glance at the address before gunning it toward Smuggler's Rest.

I make it to town in five minutes instead of ten. I slow down when I reach downtown. Hitting a pedestrian will prevent me from getting to Maya.

I park on the street near the address Paisley sent me. When I exit my truck and notice the building, I swear.

The library. I should have known Maya would come here. She's always loved this place. She spent most of her free time in high school here.

As I approach the building, the door flies open and I get a glimpse of how crowded it is inside. My stomach begins to churn. I feel as if I might vomit.

I push through the nausea. I need to get to Maya.

My hand shakes as I reach for the door. I try inhaling a deep breath to calm myself but I can't get enough air. Something is squeezing my chest.

I force myself to step inside. Luckily, I don't need to search the building. I know exactly where Maya is.

My legs tremble as I make my way past the crowd in the front room and past the rows of books to the very back of the library where there are a few private rooms. This is where Maya used to tutor me back in high school.

I have a lot of good memories from our times here. She'd make me laugh so loud we'd get in trouble with the librarian despite the closed door.

I notice my hand isn't shaking as much as I open the door to the private room where Maya is. She's huddled in her coat on a chair with a book. But she isn't reading. She's gazing out the window.

"Maya."

She startles and nearly falls off her chair. I rush to steady her. She bats my hand away.

"It's me, Caleb."

"Caleb?" The surprise in her eyes has me frowning.

"Why are you surprised I'm here?"

She shrugs and glances away.

I settle in the chair next to her. "What happened, Maya? I've been worried sick."

"Worried sick?"

"You haven't been answering your phone. No one could get in touch with you."

"No one?"

"Nova, Sophia, Chloe, and Paisley have all tried."

"I switched it off."

"Why?"

She fiddles with the edge of the desk. "I didn't want to speak to anyone."

"Why not?"

"Do we have to do this here and now?"

I nod. "I had to walk through a large crowd of people to get to you. We're sure as hell doing this here and now."

She gasps. "Oh my gosh, Caleb. I'm such a selfish cow. I didn't think." She stands. "Let's get you out of here."

I grasp her hand. "I'd prefer to wait until the library is less crowded before leaving."

"We can sneak out the back way. I haven't set off a fire alarm in ages."

I shake my head. "You can try to change the subject as often as you want, but we're not going anywhere until you tell me why you're hiding in the library."

"How do you know I'm hiding?" She waves the book she's holding at me. "This book came out today. I rushed here to be the first one to read it."

I shrug out of my coat.

Her eyes narrow. "What are you doing?"

"Settling in."

"Settling in?"

"It's obviously going to be a while before we get to the topic of why you're hiding. I might as well be comfortable. They always did keep it too warm in the library."

Her gaze darts to the door and I slide my chair back to block her exit. She can't run from me. I won't let her.

"But it's embarrassing," she whines.

"As embarrassing as having a panic attack in a crowded restaurant where everyone in town saw me?"

She scowls. "A panic attack is nothing to be embarrassed about."

"And you shouldn't be embarrassed of your parents."

She gasps. "You know?"

"All I know is you saw them." I palm her neck and squeeze. "What happened, Bunny? You can tell me anything. I won't think less of you."

I would never think less of her because of how her parents act. I love her. She's mine to protect. To cherish. To worship.

Chapter 20

"Has anyone seen a cupboard to another dimension so I can avoid this conversation?" ~ Maya

Maya

I nibble on my lip as I contemplate how to answer. I believe Caleb when he says he won't think less of me. But he doesn't know what I'm going to say. He doesn't know how unlovable I am.

"Please, tell me, Bunny." He massages my neck. "I can't help you through it if I don't know what 'it' is."

"Promise me you won't think less of me."

He crosses his heart. "I promise."

"I ran into my parents at the grocery store." I pause. I don't know how to explain what happened. When I replay the incident in my mind, it doesn't sound bad. Except it was.

"What bullshit did your mom spout this time?"

"Bullshit? How do you know what she said was bullshit? How do you know it's not true?"

He leans close and holds my gaze. "Because I know you."

"You don't know me as well as you think you do. You don't know how it was for me growing up. You don't know how they treated me."

I kept my home life separated from school. I never told anyone what happened. Sophia only found out because her brother is a cop.

Caleb leans his forehead against mine. "Please tell me what it was like for you growing up."

I know how my parents treated me wasn't my fault. I took enough psychology classes in college to figure that much out. But it's hard not to believe what they say. It's hard to feel lovable when your own flesh and blood are nasty and mean to you.

"My dad's an asshole."

Caleb's eyes flash with anger and I nearly flinch before I remember. This is Caleb. He would never physically harm me.

"What did he do?"

"He belittled me every chance he got. He made fun of me. I don't think he ever hugged me or told me he loved me growing up."

Caleb places his free hand on my thigh and squeezes. "What aren't you telling me?"

A lot.

"You can't repeat anything I say. This room is a cone of mermaid silence."

"I would never betray your confidence, Bunny." He kisses my nose. "You're mine to protect."

Those words fill me with warmth. His to protect? I can protect myself, but knowing I'm not alone is everything.

But will he feel the same way when he knows everything? I refuse to witness the disgust in his eyes when I reveal my secrets. I slam my eyes closed.

"Dad hit Mom," I rush out.

"Open your eyes, Bunny. Let me look into those gorgeous brown eyes of yours. They remind me of the finest whiskey *Buccaneer's Whiskey and Distillery* produces."

I never thought my eyes were pretty before. Brown isn't exactly exciting. Especially not considering I have my dad's eyes.

He brushes a finger over my cheek and I force my eyes open.

"Did your dad ever hit you?"

I shake my head. "No. Not after…"

"Not after what?" A muscle ticks in his jaw but his voice is devoid of anger.

"I promised I'd never tell."

"It's honorable to want to keep your promises, but keeping this secret is hurting you. And I refuse to let anything hurt you anymore."

Those words mean the world to me. This is why I love this man. He doesn't want me to hurt anymore. How could I not love him?

"I called the police on my dad. He broke Mom's arm when he pushed her down and stomped on her arm. She lied and said she fell when she went to the emergency room. I thought…" I trail off with a shake of my head.

"What did you think?"

"I was so naïve. I thought if I called the police, Mom would leave Dad and we could start over. Mom was scared of Dad. She still is. I recognize the fear in her eyes. But she wouldn't leave him. I'm the traitor for telling the police what happened. I'm the one who was kicked out of the family for daring to tell the truth. I'm the bad guy."

Caleb brushes a tear from my cheek. I didn't even realize I was crying. You'd think I'd cried enough tears for my family over the years. Apparently not.

"You are not naïve. You're brave. You're the bravest person I know."

I roll my eyes. "You faced down armed enemies. I'm not the brave one here."

"Those enemies were faceless. They meant nothing to me. It's much harder to confront a person you love. To call them out on their behavior. To call the police on a parent. Damn, Bunny. You are strong."

Goosebumps erupt all over my body. I study his eyes for any signs of deception but those blue eyes, I hope my children inherit one day, are full of honesty. "You mean it."

"Hell yeah, I mean it. You impress the hell out of me."

"But I lost my family because of what I did."

"No, you didn't."

"Mom and Dad refuse to have anything to do with me. They waited to kick me out until I was eighteen because they knew I'd tell the police if they kicked me out any earlier."

He squeezes my neck. "That egg and sperm donor are not your family. I'm your family. My family is your family. Your friends are your family. You, Maya Jenkins, are not alone in the world."

I want Caleb to be my family forever. I want to give him dozens of children. Maybe not an actual dozen but at least two. Maybe three. Probably four.

"I understand why you didn't tell me back in high school but I wish you had."

I duck my chin. "I was afraid. Dad promised he would never hit me after I told him I'd go to the police if he did. But it didn't stop him from hitting my mom or being an asshole to me. Whoever said sticks and stones may break my bones but names will never hurt me was a lying idiot."

"I hate this," Caleb grumbles. "I hate how you were suffering at home during high school and I never knew. I hate how I didn't protect you."

"I protected myself. I stayed away from home as much as possible. Why do you think I spent all my free time in the library?"

"Not all of your free time. You used to pal around with Sophia, Chloe, Nova, and Paisley. The five of you were a menace."

"My friends are the best." She glances around the library. "But this is my favorite place."

"We had a lot of good times here."

I giggle. "Because your math skills didn't improve no matter how much tutoring I gave you."

Guilt flashes in his eyes before he glances away. I gasp.

"Were you lying to me?"

He shrugs. "I may have exaggerated how bad my math skills were to get you to tutor me."

He did? Caleb Emerson – the cutest boy in high school – wanted to spend time with me?

"You could have just asked me out."

"You never went on dates. You told any boy who approached you no before they could open their mouth."

I slap his shoulder. "Because I was waiting for you to ask me, silly boy."

His hand massaging my neck freezes. "You were?"

"Duh. Why do you think I let you kiss me?"

"Because you were my friend and worried about me enlisting in the Army."

"I was worried about you enlisting. I worry about you all the time when you're away." It takes effort but I keep my gaze on his face and don't drop it to look at his injured leg. "But I wouldn't let just any boy kiss me."

His blue eyes warm. "I'm glad you let me kiss you."

I bat my eyelashes at him. "Maybe I'd let you kiss me now."

"Here? In the library? Where we could get caught?"

I bite my bottom lip. "Are you afraid, soldier boy?"

"I'm not a boy," he growls before his lips meld to mine.

I open for him and his tongue thrusts into my mouth. I cling to his shoulders as his mouth explores mine. He uses his hand on my neck to tilt my head and dives in deeper.

He lifts me up and places me on his lap. I straddle him and I can feel his hard length against my core. This is better than any kiss I've had in the library before. What am I saying? Every kiss with Caleb is better than the previous one.

Caleb's phone vibrates in his pocket and I jump at the unexpected intrusion. He ends the kiss and leans his forehead against mine as we catch our breath.

"I need to answer the phone. It could be one of your friends. They're worried about you. But make no mistake about it, we will be finishing this when we get back home."

"You won't hear me complaining."

He taps my ass and I get the hint and stand. I grab the book I was pretending to read. *How To Knit a Mermaid.* No wonder Caleb didn't believe I was reading.

"There," he says as he tucks his phone back in his pocket. "Your friends know you're safe." He holds out his hand to me. "Ready to get out of here?"

"Should I make sure the coast is clear first?"

He chuckles. "We haven't done anything wrong. We don't need to flee."

We definitely would have done something wrong if his phone hadn't beeped since nudity is not allowed in the library. There's a sign stating as much as you enter. I blame Chloe. She had a thing for streaking in public places for a while during high school.

"I'm not fleeing. I want to check there's not a big crowd at the entrance."

He squeezes my hand. "It's okay. With you by my side, the crowd won't bother me."

"I guess you better keep me by your side forever then."

"Sounds like a plan."

I was teasing but he appears serious. My breath catches in my throat. Is Caleb as serious about me as I am about him? Are all my dreams coming true?

Chapter 21

"Someone needs to give Maya's parents a lesson and I just volunteered for the job." ~ Caleb

CALEB

Where are you?

I shouldn't ignore Maya's text. But I can't tell her where I am. She'll lose her mind and come after me. And I refuse to allow her to breathe the same air as her parents any longer.

If I could kick them off this island, I would. Hell, if this doesn't work, I'll get all of Maya's friends and boyfriends together and we'll throw a 'kick the Jenkins off the island'-party. I wouldn't be surprised if all the smugglers on the island joined in.

Caleb. I'm worried.

Damnit. I can't ignore her being worried. Not after I nearly lost my mind with worry over where she was yesterday.

I'm safe.

I hit send on the message and switch my phone off. I can't have it beeping and distracting me. My task is too important.

I watch as Maya's dad drives into the garage of her parents' home. I don't wait for the garage door to shut before I step out of my truck and make my way to the front door.

I ignore the doorbell in favor of pounding on the door.

"What's your hurry?" A woman – Maya's mom I assume – shouts from inside the house.

I pound on the door again.

"I'm coming. I'm coming. Hold your freaking horses."

The door opens to reveal an older version of Maya. She has the same honey-blonde hair and pink, pouty lips Maya does. But her face is lined with wrinkles and her eyes are hard. Maya's eyes are warm and sparkle. But her mom's eyes are full of a lifetime of regret.

I understand how regret can eat away at you. But I also understand taking responsibility for your life and your decisions.

"Who are you?"

"Invite me in," I order.

"I'm not inviting someone I don't know into my house." She rakes her gaze over me. "Hold on. Are you Caleb?" Her eyes light with recognition. "You sure grew up well."

"Invite me in," I insist between grit teeth.

She sweeps a hand toward the interior of the house. "Come in. Come in."

I enter and follow her into the living room. I take a moment to study the home Maya grew up in. The furniture appears expensive with its classic design and leather fabrics, but it also looks brand new as if it's never been used.

The entire room reminds me of a display in a furniture store. Everything is perfect. There are no depressions from people sitting on the couch, no drinks left out, no blankets to cuddle under. It's cold and clinical.

"Geraldine," Maya's father bellows as he enters the house from the garage.

Geraldine startles and I scowl. She's obviously afraid of her own husband. Why the hell doesn't she leave him?

"We have a visitor, Roger."

Roger walks into the living room and smiles at me. His smile is fake as shit. "Who's our visitor, Geraldine?"

He moves to his wife and wraps an arm around her to pull her near. She winces when he touches her hip. I nearly lose my hold on my temper but I reign it in. I have a message to send to these people. Ranting and screaming won't help.

"This is Caleb," Geraldine says. "Caleb, this is my husband, Roger."

Roger holds out his hand but I cross my arms over my chest. No way am I shaking the hand of the man who tortured the woman I love throughout her childhood.

"Ah, yes, I remember you," he says as he drops his hand. "What can we do for you today?"

"You can stop harassing Maya."

He chuckles. "She's our child. We don't harass her."

"I was being kind using the word harass. You will stop torturing your daughter."

His eyes narrow. I know the look. I've seen enough evil men in my time in the Army to recognize evil when I come across it. This man is rotten through and through.

"It's none of your business."

I snort. "You tried to make it none of my business. You convinced me I wasn't good enough for your daughter. But you didn't give a shit if I was good enough for her or not. You just didn't want her to be happy. You want her to be miserable the same way you are."

"What is he talking about?" Geraldine asks Roger. "You convinced Caleb he wasn't good enough for Maya?"

Apparently, she doesn't know about the 'talk' her husband had with me.

Roger shrugs. "It's true, isn't it? He's a soldier. He's not even an officer."

He doesn't have the first clue what he's talking about. I could be an officer if I wanted to. I got my degree a few years back. But I'm not letting him derail this conversation. This discussion is not about me. It never was.

"You are the ones who aren't good enough for Maya," I grumble. "You're the ones who shouldn't breathe the same air as her."

"I don't know who you think you are but—"

I hold up my hand to stop his tantrum. This isn't a discussion.

"From now on, Maya doesn't exist for you. You don't call her. You don't speak to her. You leave her the hell alone."

Geraldine rolls her eyes. "We live in a small town on a small island, we can't help but run into *our daughter* once in a while."

Their daughter? How dare she! They never treated Maya like a daughter. They didn't love her and cherish her the way they should have. They didn't nurture her the way a child needs. Their mistreatment of Maya stops now.

"You bump into Maya at the grocery store, you walk away. You bump into her at a restaurant, you turn around. And you sure as shit don't search for her anywhere."

Roger prowls toward me. A muscle ticks in his jaw and his eyes are full of fire. If he's trying to intimidate me, he's going to have to try a fuck of a lot harder.

"You!" He shakes his finger at me. "You don't tell me what to do. Who the hell do you think you are? Do you know who I am?"

"I know exactly the kind of man you are. The kind that isn't a man at all. The kind that thinks hitting a woman makes him strong. The kind that thinks putting other people down makes him bigger. Clue in – you aren't the big man. You're a small man in a big man's clothes who doesn't know how to wear them."

"How dare you?" He raises his fist.

I lift my eyebrow. "Gonna hit me? Go ahead. This should be fun."

His nostrils flare as he shakes his fist in the air. "Get out of here!" Spit flies from his mouth as he yells. "Get out of here! And don't ever come back!"

"Trust me. I don't ever want to come back to this emotionless mausoleum. But I will if you don't heed my warning. Stay the hell away from Maya. She's no longer your daughter. She's nothing to you."

"Get out! Get out!" Roger's eyes are bulging. I wouldn't be surprised if he pops a blood vessel in his eye.

I glance over my shoulder at Maya's mom as I make my way to the door. Roger is going to lose it on her once I'm gone.

Shit. I can't abandon her here with him but there's no way she'll go anywhere with me. She refused to accept the helping hand Maya offered her. She sure as hell isn't accepting help from me.

I'll phone the cops. It's the only recourse I have.

When I open the door, I realize I don't have to contact anyone since there's a cop waiting on the porch.

I hold up my hands. "I didn't touch him."

He smirks. "I wouldn't blame you if you did."

My brow wrinkles. "What?"

He chuckles and holds out his hand. "I'm Weston. I'm Sophia's brother."

Now I understand why he appears familiar. Weston and I had a few interactions when he was a rookie cop and I was a shithead teenager. Although, he's changed over the decade I've been gone. But, then, so have I.

"I'm doing a welfare check." He winks before knocking on the door.

"Go away!" Roger shouts from inside the house.

"Go on." Weston nods to my truck. "Get out of here. I've got this."

"How did you know I was here?"

He taps his nose. "A little bunny told me."

Crap. Maya knows I'm here. She's probably losing her mind.

"Thanks, man. I didn't consider Maya's mom's safety."

"Don't you dare feel guilty. Maya's been carrying that guilt around for years. It's not her guilt to carry and it's certainly not yours. You did right by her. It's about damn time."

"Yes, it is," I mutter.

I climb into my truck and switch on my phone. It immediately starts beeping with message after message from Maya. I scroll to the last one.

Don't do anything stupid.

She probably won't agree with me, but I didn't do anything stupid. I did what needed to be done. And if her parents ignore my warnings, I'll do what I need to do to get my point across. Maya's life will no longer be poisoned by her egg and sperm donor.

They are not her family.

I am.

Chapter 22

"When all else fails, call a cop." ~ *words Maya never thought she'd say*

MAYA

I study the message from Caleb.

I'm safe.

Those words do not reassure me at all. Quite the opposite in fact. My hackles are raised and I'm terrified he's off doing dangerous deeds – such as confronting my parents.

He was beyond angry yesterday when I confessed what I endured at home while growing up. Should I not have told him? Should I have kept my past a secret?

I send another message.

Don't do anything stupid.

I wait but there's no blue tick to reassure me my message has been sent. He must have switched his phone off.

What do I do now? I could drive to my parents' house and check if he's there. I snatch my keys from the side table but halt in front of the door.

I need to calm down. Driving off half-cocked will not help the situation. I don't even know if Caleb is at my parents' house. For all I know he's at physical therapy and doesn't want me to know. He's super secretive about his sessions. I'm still unaware of the extent of his injuries.

I do the next best thing, I dial Weston's number. Sophia's brother is the cop I called when Dad broke Mom's arm. He knows what it was like for me growing up.

"What's up, Maya?"

"Um...I need your help."

"What is it? Are you hurt? Do you need an ambulance?"

My eyes widen in surprise. Usually, when I ring Weston, he's worried what trouble I'm in and how much bail money I need. Things have changed since he found Scarlett and fell in love.

Their love story was more exciting than a romance book. They got snowed in with no electricity at Christmas. I bet I know how they kept each other warm.

I shake those thoughts out of my mind. I need to worry about my own love story now.

"No. No. No. I'm fine. I need you to check on Caleb."

"What's wrong? What happened? Did you get in a fight? Is he having another anxiety attack?"

"You know about those?"

"Darling, it's a small island. Everyone knows about Caleb's anxiety attack at *Smuggler's Cove*."

"He's embarrassed. Please don't tell him you know."

"You can count on me, Maya. Now, why do I need to check on him? Where is he?"

"I think he's at my parents."

"You told him?" He whistles. "Good for you, Maya. Proud of you, little sis."

His words warm my heart but I don't have time for this. "Can you check if he's there? And whether I need bail money?"

"You won't need bail money," he growls. "Don't you worry. I've got this."

He hangs up before I can thank him. It's fine. Everything's fine. There's no need to worry. Weston will find Caleb before any blood is spilled. I hope.

I pace the living room of the cabin as I wait for Caleb to return. My phone beeps with a message from Weston.

Caleb is on his way home to you.

Thank the mermaids swimming in the sea! He's coming home.

Not ten minutes later, headlights from his truck shine through the front window. I rush to the door and fling it open before running down the steps to his truck.

As soon as Caleb is out of his truck, I throw myself at him.

"I was worried."

He wraps his arms around me and holds me close. "I'm okay, Bunny. I'm okay."

I lean back to meet his gaze. "Where did you go? What happened? Are you injured?"

"I think you know where I went since you sent Weston after me."

I raise my eyebrows. "Would you have preferred I came myself?"

He growls. "Fuck no."

"What happened? Please don't make me regret confessing my secrets to you."

His blue eyes darken until they're nearly black. "You never need to regret confessing your secrets to me. I'll be your secret keeper."

"Except you went to visit my parents after I told you my secrets."

He frowns at me. "You're shivering. Let's go inside."

I allow him to lead me inside where we settle on the sofa, but I'm not done pressuring him.

"Why did you visit my parents? What happened?"

He grasps my hands and lifts them to kiss my knuckles. "I ordered them to stay away from you."

"Stay away from me? I don't understand. They're my parents."

"No, they're not. Those people were never your parents."

"But…" I bite my bottom lip. "It's my mom and dad."

He cradles my face with his palms. "No, Bunny, they aren't. They never were."

My chest feels tight and my vision blurs. Geraldine gave birth to me. She was supposed to love me unconditionally. Roger is my dad. He was supposed to protect me from all the bad things in the world. Not become the bad thing I needed protection from.

Caleb brushes the hair off of my forehead. "I need to tell you something. It's going to hurt, but you need to know the truth."

Help me smugglers. What now?

"Are you ready?"

"I don't think I'll ever be ready to hear whatever you're going to say."

"I'm here, Maya. I'm not going anywhere."

All the coldness, thoughts of my parents caused, is banished by his words.

"Okay." I nod. "I'm ready."

"There's a reason I never asked you out when we were in high school."

I know. We discussed this yesterday. "You thought I'd say no."

"I did but I knew I could convince you to say yes."

I would have said yes right away. No convincing needed. "Then, why didn't you ask me?"

"Your dad."

"My dad? What does my dad have to do with us?"

Caleb squeezes my neck. "Hear me out."

I blow out a breath. "Okay."

"After one of our study sessions at the library, I was walking home and ran into your dad. It wasn't an accident. He was looking for me."

My dad sought Caleb out? What in the world? I bite my tongue before I interrupt.

"He forbade me from dating you. He said you were meant for greater things than this small town on this little island. He told me I was not man enough for you. And, in case I wasn't convinced, he said he wouldn't give you your college fund money if I dated you."

I gasp. "My college fund money? My parents never gave me any money for college. I got scholarships and worked as a waitress. They didn't give me a dime."

He growls. "They didn't?"

"Nope. This doesn't make any sense. Mom and Dad thought I was too big for my britches. They never said a nice word to me. And then, all of sudden, Dad's telling you I'm meant for greater things? What a lying piece of smuggler's reject whiskey."

I jump to my feet and begin pacing the room. "How dare he say you weren't man enough for me! You're the best man I've ever known." I stop pacing to stare down at him. "Please tell me you didn't join the Army to become a better man."

He shrugs and I explode.

"No! I lost over a decade with you because of my dad. All that time. All those years. All those lonely Christmas days. New Year's Eves spent alone. And for what?"

I don't bother to try and stop my tears. There's no chance of stopping them considering the destruction my father caused.

"I knew my dad was an asshole but to ruin my life?"

Caleb wraps his arms around me and sways me from side to side. "I hate to say it, Maya, but I think ruining your life was the purpose of his little talk with me."

I shove him away. "What? My own father tried to ruin my life?"

"He is not your father. Or your dad. He's nothing to you. He's your past. One you are not going to dwell on."

"I'm not going to dwell on?" I slap my hand over my heart. "What do you expect me to do?"

He grasps my hands and hauls me near. "I expect you to live your life with me. I expect you to let me protect you from any further bullshit they try to pull from now on. I expect you to be my family."

It sounds nice but, "It's not going to be easy."

He tucks a strand of hair behind my ear. "Nothing worth having is easy, Bunny. Will you at least try?"

"You want me to give up on my parents."

"Bunny, they're not worthy of being your parents."

"It hurts." I feel as if my heart is tearing into little pieces and will never be whole again. "The people who should love me unconditionally don't love me at all."

"That's on them. Not you."

"Easy for you to say. Your family is awesome."

"They're your family now, too."

Wow. He's giving me everything I've ever wanted. "You're making it hard for me to say no."

He waggles his eyebrows. "I'll make it worth your while."

Hang the smugglers. I can't deny him.

Maybe he's right. Maybe I need to stop yearning for my parents' love. Maybe it's time to face reality. My dad tried to ruin my life. Maybe he'll never love me.

"I'll try."

He smiles and his dimple makes an appearance. I should make him smile more often because he doesn't smile enough. He used to smile all the time as a teenager.

"Thank you, Bunny. You won't regret this."

I open my mouth to ask him how he's going to make it up to me but he picks me up and throws me over his shoulder before I have a chance to speak.

"Talking time is over. Time to show you how much I appreciate you taking a chance on me."

I won't say no to his idea.

I don't know if I'll ever be able to cut myself off from my parents but if this is my reward for trying, I'm going to try.

Chapter 23

"Maya drives me wild. I'm never letting her go." ~ Caleb

CALEB

I lay Maya down on the bed and cover her with my body. This is where she belongs. In my bed – with me – forever. I nearly told her I love her. But I didn't want my declaration of love to influence her decision. She needs to realize her parents aren't worth her love on her own.

But I'm done thinking about those pieces of shit. I have a warm, willing woman beneath me. The woman I've always wanted but thought I couldn't have.

So many years lost. Years I could have spent with my bunny. Years we could have spent building our family.

I force those thoughts away and concentrate on Maya. She flutters her lashes at me and bites her bottom lip. My shy girl becomes a temptress in the bed. I fucking love it.

I pull her lip from her teeth. "Don't harm my lip."

"I think it's my lip."

"When we're in this bed. Together. It's mine." I punch my hips and press my hard length into her stomach and she gasps. "You're mine."

She winds her arms around my neck. "And you're mine."

"Always, Bunny. Always."

I crash my lips to hers and she opens on a sigh. Her honey taste hits me and I moan. I love her taste. I love her. Plain and simple.

I need to tell her how I feel but not yet. Not when we're in bed and my cock is begging for release. I don't want her to think my declaration is a result of sexual frenzy.

I explore her mouth with my tongue as my hands skim up and down her sides. She squirms beneath me and I end the kiss to smile down at her.

"Is there something you want?"

"Yep."

"You gonna tell me what it is?"

She wraps her legs around my hips and rubs her core against my hard length. "You're a smart man. I think you can figure it out for yourself."

Damn. She's cute.

She's also causing my cock to weep in anticipation.

I grasp her thigh to stop her movements. "Keep it up and this is going to be over before it begins."

She bats her eyelashes at me. "Do you not have enough stamina, soldier?"

I growl. "I have stamina. But you're a temptress."

Her eyes light with happiness. "I'm a temptress?" She giggles.

I nip her bottom lip. "To me, you are."

"What are you going to do about it?" She wiggles her hips against my hard length and I bite back a moan.

"I'm going to fuck you until you see stars," I grumble.

I planned to make love to Maya. Show her how much I love her without saying the words. But my cock has other plans.

"I don't know. Maybe you can't make me see stars."

"I do love a challenge."

"When does this challenge begin, soldier?"

"Right, the hell now."

I get to my knees and unwrap her legs from my waist. I snap her jeans open and shove my hand inside. I skip her clit and go straight for her pussy. I plunge two fingers inside.

"You're already wet for me."

"Mm-hm."

I begin to pump in and out of her. She arches her back in a silent plea for more. She's gorgeous with her cheeks flushed and her pouty lips gaping open. But I want more.

"Lift up your sweater."

She doesn't hesitate to follow directions. She yanks her sweater up to reveal her black bra.

"Pull your tits out."

She tugs the cups down to reveal her breasts.

"Play with yourself. Play with those pretty titties while I work this pussy."

She begins to pluck at her nipples. "Oh god," she moans.

I stop and her eyes fly open. "Not god. Caleb. You say my name when you come."

Her walls flutter around my fingers. My shy girl loves it when I talk dirty. I bet it's because her 'romance' novels are actually full of smut. Maybe I should have her act out some of those scenes. But in the meantime...

"Are you going to come for me, Bunny?"

She bobs her head. Not good enough. I want her wild and desperate to come. I increase the speed of my thrusts.

"Is your pussy going to squeeze my fingers?"

She moans.

"Are you going to soak my fingers?"

Her walls tighten around me.

"Remember to scream my name when you come."

I grind my palm against her clit as I pound into her. Her mouth falls open and her head flies back as her orgasm strikes.

"Say. My. Name."

"C-c-caleb."

I slow my thrusts until her body collapses on the bed. I trace her mouth with my finger.

"Open up. I want you to taste yourself."

Her eyes fly open. She hesitates for a moment before opening her mouth. I tap her lip with my fingers and she sucks on them.

"Like the sweetest honey," I murmur.

"I bet you taste better."

I frown. If she sucks me off, she won't miss the scars on my leg. I'm not ready to show those to her yet.

"Next time," I say.

She pouts. "You never let me touch you or taste you."

I cover her with my body. "Did you not enjoy what we just did?"

"You know I did but I want more."

I punch my hips into her stomach. "And you'll get more."

"Will you take off your clothes this time?"

I start to say no but stop. It's not fair of me to keep this part of me secret. Not after Maya told me all of her secrets. And especially not after I made her promise to stop yearning for her parents' love.

But I'm not ready. I need to make sure she's so firmly attached to me, she won't go running into the ocean to join the mermaids when she sees my skin. My scars are not a pretty sight.

"Please," she pleas. "I want to see you."

I give in. Sort of. "Shirt off. Pants on."

She waggles her eyebrows. "But the pants are the best part."

I grind my hard length into her stomach. "Don't worry. You'll get the best part."

I crawl off of the bed. I stand at the end and remove her jeans and panties.

"Sweater and bra off."

She whips both the garments off and now she's completely bare to me. Millions and millions of miles of smooth skin to explore on her curvy body.

"Your turn." She waves to my shirt.

I whip it off and she gasps.

"Wow. Good thing there aren't any mermaids around or they'd steal you away from me with their siren song."

She completely ignores the jagged scar across my pec. Did she not notice it? I study her face for clues. She's biting her bottom lip while her wide eyes are glued to my chest. She really doesn't care.

Maybe she won't care about my leg. Maybe the scars and mottled skin won't bother her. No. I can't chance it. Not yet.

"Mermaids can't live outside of the water," I say instead.

She wags her finger at me. "You're forgetting the legend of the mermaid."

I grasp her ankle and yank her body to me. She yelps. "Do you want to discuss mermaids or do you want me to fuck you?"

She taps her chin and pretends to consider the question. "Um…"

I pinch her nipple and she moans. "Do I need to ask the question again?"

She shakes her head. "Nope. Fuck me. The answer is definitely fuck me."

The sound of her saying fuck while naked on my bed causes my cock to twitch. Its patience is gone as is mine.

I unzip my jeans and take out my cock. I wrap her legs around my waist and notch my cock at her entrance. I inch inside. Her wet heat surrounds me and I moan.

"Fuck."

Maya's eyes fly open. "What's wrong?"

"Condom. I need to get a condom."

"No need. I'm on the pill." She bites her bottom lip. "Although, Nova got pregnant while she was on birth control, so maybe you don't want to chance me getting pregnant."

The image of her belly round with my baby flashes into my mind. I want it. I want her. I want children with her. A family. All of it. I want it all.

"I'm clean, too. I got a full medical work up when…"

When I was in the hospital recovering from being shot. I need to tell her about my injury. About the future. But not yet. Not until she's addicted to me. Not until she can't live without me. The way I can't live without her.

Maya wiggles her ass. "What are you waiting for?"

For her to bitch about me keeping secrets. But when I gaze into her eyes, they're not filled with questions or concerns. Only heat and warmth.

I sink into her. I've never been inside a woman without a condom before. Never wanted to before.

But since I've had Maya without one. We're not going back.

This woman is mine and I'm going to give her babies someday.

Chapter 24

"My new assignment is to not dwell on the past. I'm probably gonna fail." ~ *Maya*

MAYA

I sigh as I wake. I'm surrounded by Caleb's warm and earthy scent. This is what I've always wanted. What I've dreamed of since the first time I tutored him in math.

And I finally have it. Although, I could have had this for over a decade. If it weren't for my dad.

Caleb kisses my neck. "How are you feeling about everything?"

"I'm mad at Dad for lying to you. I'm upset we lost all of these years together. I'm sad to give up on ever being the recipient of my parents' love."

His arm around me tightens. "I'm sorry, Maya. I should have told you what your dad said at the time but I didn't want to hurt you."

I squeeze his hand. "I don't blame you. It's not your fault. The fault lies entirely with him."

"Try not to dwell on your anger."

I snort. "Not dwell on my anger? What do you want me to do instead? Be devastated because my parents don't love me. I know they never loved me. But I thought…" I sigh. "It doesn't matter what I thought."

Caleb rolls me around until we're facing each other. "Bunny, what you think matters."

My nose wrinkles. "Even if what I'm thinking is how to convince you to drive to *Pirates Pastries* to buy me some goodies for breakfast?"

He chuckles. "I'll buy you whatever you want, but you're not getting out of this conversation."

"When did you become this tenacious?"

He lays his palm on my cheek. "When I met this adorable seven-year-old with honey-blonde hair and whiskey-colored eyes on the monkey bars."

My heart flips in my chest. "You remember?"

"Of course, I remember. How could I forget? You were terrified but the second you were safely on the ground, you ran off to your girlfriends to plot against those bullies. As I recall, they ended up with mud on the butt of their pants. Everyone thought they'd shit their pants."

"It was Chloe's idea. She always has the best ideas."

He taps my nose. "Now tell me what you were thinking about your parents."

I sigh. He's not going to let this go. I fiddle with the hem of his t-shirt. "It sounds stupid."

He pinches my chin to lift my face. I meet his gaze. "Nothing you say could ever sound stupid."

"You obviously haven't met drunk Maya yet."

"I can't wait to meet her. Now, stop stalling."

I blow out a breath. "I thought if we made *Five Fathoms Brewing* into a success, my parents might start to speak to me again. We'd slowly reconnect and eventually, they'd learn to love me. Told you. It's stupid."

He wraps his arms around me and hauls me to him. I bury my face in his chest.

"It's not stupid. Wanting your parents to love you is normal. I have no idea how you became this amazing woman I love considering how they treated you."

I shrug. "I…" Hold on. What did he say? I lean back to gaze up at him. "Did you say, 'woman you love'?"

"Nope. I said, 'amazing woman I love'."

My mouth gapes open. "You love me?"

He chuckles. "Isn't it obvious? I came back to Smuggler's Hideaway determined to hide away from everyone – you and my family included – because I thought everyone in my life was better off without me. And yet you barreled your way inside this cabin in no time."

"I wouldn't say barreled my way."

"And I managed to keep our relationship fake for about a second."

"It was definitely more than a second."

He smiles down at me. "I love you, Maya."

"Phew. What a relief."

He tickles my ribs. "Why is it a relief?"

I slap his hands away. "Duh. Because I love you, too. I've loved you since high school. I was devastated when you left to join the Army. I thought you'd be gone a few years. Not twelve. At least you wrote back when I started writing you letters. I worried you'd ignore me."

He lays his forehead against mine. "I could never ignore you. Those letters were my lifeline."

Heat radiates throughout my chest. "Your lifeline?"

"They kept me sane. Whenever I thought I couldn't run another mile or sleep another night in the sand, I'd re-read your letters." He smirks. "Plus, those care packages you sent made me the most popular guy in my platoon."

"I wish I would have sent you more."

"Bunny, you sent a care package practically once a month."

"The postal workers all know me by name."

He rolls his eyes. "This is Smuggler's Hideaway. They already knew who you were."

Speaking of Smuggler's Hideaway. "Why didn't you ever come home before? Your family met up with you in Germany a few times but you never came home. Why?"

He glances away. "I was being stupid."

"Only I get to say when you're being stupid. Tell me why and I'll render my verdict."

"I was afraid to see you."

Those words stab my heart and fill my veins with ice. Caleb – the man I was obsessed with – was afraid to see me. "You were afraid of me?"

"Not afraid of you." He presses a quick kiss to my lips. "I could never be afraid of you."

"Are you saying I'm a wimp?"

"I'm saying I was afraid if I saw you, I wouldn't be able to resist you."

Oh. This I can handle. I waggle my eyebrows. "I am pretty irresistible. But why would you want to resist me?"

"I didn't want to screw up your life."

"Screw up my life by giving me love and affection?"

"Told you I was being stupid."

"It's over now." I blow out a breath. "We need to stop dwelling on the past and move forward."

"Agreed." Caleb caresses my turquoise bracelet. "I can't believe you kept this all this time."

"Of course, I kept it. You gave it to me for my twenty-first birthday. The only gift you gave me by the way. You owe me a bunch of gifts." So much for not dwelling on the past anymore.

"I do, do I?"

"Yep. I'm keeping track. I've given you birthday gifts every year for the past twelve years. You've given me one. You owe me eleven gifts."

"Can I pay you back in orgasms?"

My nipples tighten at the promise in his voice but I feign indifference. "You're going to give me orgasms anyway."

He twirls a strand of my hair around his finger. "Maybe you could get some of those smutty books you read out and we can reenact the best scenes."

I sniff and stick my nose in the air. "I'll have you know not all my romance books are smutty."

He smirks. "But some of them are."

I can't deny it. Some of them are more than a bit smutty. A girl's gotta eat when the man she's obsessed with is overseas fighting enemies.

"But you're not an alien or a werewolf."

He nibbles on my jaw. "I'm happy to bite you."

"And there's only one of you. There's no way we can recreate a reverse harem sexy scene with just the two of us."

"We will not be partaking in threesomes or orgies. I'm all you need." He twists my nipple and I rub my thighs together to relieve the tension he's building.

"Orgasms don't count as birthday gifts," I gasp out.

"Too bad," he mutters. "Because I'd get at least three years of gifts taken care of this morning."

"T-t-three?"

He shrugs. "Maybe four."

I cling to his t-shirt. "No way can you give me four orgasms in one morning."

His blue eyes sparkle. "But I can try." He sneaks his hands under my t-shirt and begins lifting the fabric off of me. "Unless you don't want to? Unless you'd rather have a shipwreck cookie from *Pirates Pastries?*"

"I want four orgasms *and* a shipwreck cookie. Maybe a baked peaches and cream whiskey muffin, too."

He chuckles. "Are you ordering orgasms?"

I raise my eyebrows. "Unless you can't deliver."

"Don't you worry. I can deliver everything I promise and more."

"Love you, my sexy soldier."

"And I love you, Bunny." My chest fills with warmth at his words. I could float away on a cloud.

He kisses my nose. "Now, take off your clothes."

Forget about the cloud. My body tingles in anticipation. I giggle as I wiggle out of my panties.

"Four orgasms," I remind him.

"Don't you worry. I'll give you one with my mouth. One with my fingers. And two with my cock."

I shiver.

"On your back. Spread your legs. You're coming on my tongue first."

Oh goodie. "You say the sweetest things."

Caleb settles between my thighs and I forget all about the heavy stuff. The years we lost together. The fear I'm unlovable. All of it is wiped from my mind as his tongue finds my clit and he sucks.

I thread my hands through his hair and hold on for the ride.

I don't plan to ever let go. I'm in this through thick and thin. Because Caleb is mine. My person. My love. My family.

Chapter 25

"If they're not loud and obnoxious, are they really family?" ~ Maya

Maya

I tug on Caleb's hand until he stops walking up the driveway to Sophia's mom's house. "Are you sure about this?"

He motions to the window where my friends are watching us from behind the curtains. Nosy but not very stealthy. "A bit late for backing out now."

"No, it isn't. You're under no obligation to attend drunk poker."

My friends and I play drunk poker once a month at Sophia's parents' house. Lily, Sophia's mom, tried to get everyone to come over for Sunday dinner once a month but people would bail on her. No one bails on drunk poker.

"You want to go home? We're out of here in a flash."

"A flash? Do you have an outfit for the Flash as well?"

My cheeks warm. I may have shown him my Little Red Riding Hood costume last night. It was not a child's costume.

"You'll never find out if you continue to tease me."

"Oh, Bunny, I will tease you and you're going to love it."

I shiver as heat shoots from my belly straight to my core where my panties dampen.

Caleb's blue eyes sparkle. "Maybe I want to go home now and tease you."

The door to the house flies open and Sophia steps outside. "Get your butts in here."

Chloe elbows her. "No fair. I bet they wouldn't come inside."

I glance up at Caleb. "Are you sure you want to spend an evening with my friends?"

"Of course, I do. They're your family."

My family? I study my girlfriends who are now all waiting on the porch. Is Caleb correct? Are Paisley, Nova, Chloe, and Sophia my family?

"I'd run if I were you," Weston says as he comes up behind us with his girlfriend, Scarlett, on his arm.

Scarlett slaps him. "Don't listen to him." She addresses Caleb. "He bet you wouldn't stay."

"I'm done with this." I stomp to the front door. "None of you will make bets about whether Caleb stays anymore. Do you hear me?"

My friends stare at me with their eyes wide.

"I said. Do you hear me?"

"Thank the smugglers, Maya found her voice," Sophia mutters.

"She always had a voice. She just doesn't choose to use it often," Paisley adds.

My nostrils flare and my heart pounds. They aren't listening to me. They don't understand. Caleb has a hard enough time coming out in public and being in crowds. They're jerks for making bets about it.

Caleb wraps an arm around my shoulders. "It's okay, Maya. There's no need to be angry."

I whirl around to face him. "Yes, there is! Someone needs to protect you and I've accepted the position."

He chuckles as he brushes the hair off of my forehead to kiss me. "Thanks, but I'm good."

I study his face. He's not sweating, there are no tremors, and he's breathing normally.

"Okay." I nod. "But if anything changes, let me know."

"You got it, Flash."

Lily makes her way to the front of the group. "What's going on? Why is everyone standing outside?"

Weston motions to Sophia. "My sister is blocking the way."

"I'm not blocking the way. Unless you're too scared to go past me."

Lily sighs. "Children. Can we not fight today?"

Sophia points at Weston. "He started it."

Lily slashes her hand in the air. "I don't care who started it. It ends now. This is a family gathering and we have a new family member. Let's be on our best behavior."

Chloe barks out a laugh. "Caleb knows us. We went to high school with him."

Caleb groans. "Don't remind me. I still haven't recovered from the time the five of you decided to streak across the gym at a pep rally while the cheerleaders were doing their routine."

Nova scowls. "They shouldn't have tried to ban us from cheerleading for life."

"They didn't ban me," Paisley declares. "They banned *you* after the incident."

Nova rolls her eyes. "The 'incident'. You make it sound as if people died."

"There were broken bones," Paisley says.

Nova glares at her. "Don't be mean just because Eli has your panties in a twist."

Paisley growls. "My panties are not in a twist over some jerk from high school."

Lily throws her hands in the air. "I give up. You're all heathens. I tried my best." She shackles my wrist. "Come help me in the kitchen."

I allow her to lead me into the house but glance over my shoulder at Caleb. *You okay?*

He lifts his chin in response.

"Holy smugglers," I mutter when we reach the kitchen and I notice the amount of food on the counters. "How many people are you expecting?"

"With all of my girls falling in love, I have more men to feed."

Her girls? Lily only has one daughter – Sophia. "Your girls?"

She rolls her eyes. "Sophia, Chloe, Nova, and now you."

Oh.

"You do realize I consider you one of my own, don't you?"

"Sure," I lie.

She sighs but doesn't call me on my lie. "How are you doing after the grocery store incident?"

I groan. "Does everyone know what happened?"

"It's Smuggler's Hideaway."

In other words, yes, everyone knows.

"I've waited years for you to come talk to me about your parents."

My nose wrinkles. "You have?"

She grasps my hands and squeezes. "Yes, darling girl. I wanted to be there for you, but I didn't want to pressure you. I'm afraid I was wrong. I should have pressured you."

I'm confused. Don't get me wrong. Sophia's mom has always been supportive. She was the mom of our friend group who always had cookies ready for us after school. And, when we got older, she let us hang out in the basement.

It was in her very basement where I tried moonshine for the very first time. She was also the one who held my hair while I threw moonshine up for the very first time. And she helped me when I had my first period. When I...

Mermaid's bells. Lily has been there all along. When my mother wouldn't talk to me about boys, Lily sat me down and gave me the sex talk. It was very detailed. And informative. And probably a bit too early since I decided sex was not for me afterwards.

When I had trouble with a teacher who thought I cheated on a test, it was Lily who went to the school and discussed the problem. When I cried because bullies were teasing me, it was Lily who held my hand and explained the best way to deal with them.

Tears well in my eyes and my bottom lip wobbles. "I-I-I didn't realize."

Lily folds me into her arms and hugs me up tight. "No need to cry, darling girl."

The kitchen door bangs open and I'm wrenched from Lily's arms. "What's wrong?" Caleb growls. "You made my Maya cry."

"Oh my. All of my girls found big, strapping men to love them."

I giggle as I push away from Caleb. "It's okay, soldier boy. Lily was asking me about my parents is all."

He scowls. "They are not your parents. Geraldine is your egg donor. And Roger is your sperm donor. They biologically created you but they are not the people who raised you."

Lily smiles. "You chose well, Maya. You chose well."

"Yeah," I say as I meet Caleb's gaze. I probably have cartoon hearts in my eyes at the moment. "I did."

She claps her hands. "Help me get this food onto the table before the masses riot."

Caleb frowns at the trays of fried chicken, nachos, cheese and crackers, mini quiches, and veggies. "I thought we were playing poker."

I elbow him. "We're playing drunk poker."

"What's the difference?"

"You'll see," I sing.

We carry the plates of food into the dining room where the dining table has been transformed into a poker table. Lily follows us carrying a tray with shots of moonshine. She hands them out and holds up her glass.

"To the smugglers, bootleggers, rumrunners…"

"And mermaids who loved them!" We finish the toast before knocking back our shots.

Caleb winces. "I forgot how strong Smuggler's Hideaway moonshine is. At least it's tastier than the shit we distilled in our barracks in the desert."

"I'm going to need to buy a new table," Lily says as she sits across from us. "We don't have room for Paisley's man."

Paisley scowls. "I don't have a man."

"What about Eli?" Sophia teases.

"Say Eli's name one more time and you'll find out just how good my chemistry skills are."

Lily clears her throat. "I meant once you find your man."

"Or harem of men," Chloe mutters. "Remember the time Lily found her watching an orgy?"

Weston groans. "Stop. I don't want to hear about my sisters having sex. It's bad enough my best friend is engaged to my sister."

"And now Nova is engaged to Hudson," Paisley says.

I gasp. "What?"

Nova waves with her left hand, which is now sporting a diamond engagement ring.

I jump up to give her a hug. "I'm so happy for you. All your dreams are coming true."

"So are yours," she whispers back to me.

I hope so. I release her and return to my seat to give everyone else a chance to congratulate her.

"When did this happen?" I ask once everyone's returned to their seats. "And why did Paisley know?"

"I know because I'm observant," Paisley says.

"I noticed her ring but thought everyone already knew," Weston says.

Sophia rolls her eyes at him. "Sure, you did."

Weston steals a quiche from her plate and pops it in his mouth. She slaps him but he laughs before jumping up from the table and running away. Sophia chases after him.

I lean close to Caleb. "You okay?"

"Fine."

"This group can get rowdy."

"They're your family. I expected rowdy."

"I'm not rowdy."

"Says the girl who highjacked the PA from the high school principal to announce her bullies all wet the bed until they were in junior high."

I gasp. "No one was supposed to know it was me."

"Bunny, I always knew where you were in high school."

I sigh. "We missed so many years together."

He kisses my nose. "But we're not going to dwell on those lost years now. We're going to enjoy our evening with your family."

I glance around the room. Sophia is chasing Weston while Scarlett yells at him to stop running. Nova and Hudson are shouting at everyone to be quiet since the baby's sleeping in Sophia's childhood bedroom. Chloe's telling anyone who will listen how they all owe her an apology since everyone assumed she was behind the PA stunt.

My gaze lands on Lily who winks at me.

Warmth fills me. This is my family. My parents aren't my family. They haven't been for a long time. I need to stop yearning for their love.

I'm going to try. Starting today.

Chapter 26

"If Maya wants me to act out her lumberjack fantasies, I'm all in. And I do mean in." ~ Caleb

CALEB

"No fair," Maya pouts.

"What?"

She waves her hand up and down my outfit. I glance down at what I'm wearing. I'm in a pair of jeans and a flannel shirt. I don't understand what the big deal is.

"You're going to chop wood and I have to go to work."

I scratch my head. "You're upset I'm going to chop wood?"

"No. I'm upset you're going to chop wood and I don't get to watch."

I waggle my eyebrows. "If you stay and watch, I'll take my shirt off."

Her eyes flare and I step toward her. The wood can wait. I wrap an arm around her waist and haul her near.

She looks up at me from beneath her lashes. "It's a tempting offer."

"Let me sweeten the pot," I murmur before I touch my lips to hers. I trace her bottom lip with my tongue. "Let me in, Bunny."

She opens on a sigh and I thrust my tongue into her mouth. Her honey taste hits me and I moan. I'm quickly becoming addicted to the taste. I'll never get enough of it. I want to taste it every day for the rest of my life.

She clings to my shoulders and I grasp her hips to lift her up. She wraps her legs around my hips and—

Her phone beeps.

She disengages from me and rushes to her phone. She reads the message and swears under her breath. "I need to go. The Gourmet Corner grocery store representatives are visiting today, and Paisley is freaking out about them entering her brewery."

She runs around in circles as she searches for her coat, keys, and bag. I stand at the door and jingle her keys.

She rushes to me and snatches them. "Thank you. I'll be home late." She rushes out the door but skids to a halt and whirls back around. "I mean back at the cabin late. This isn't my home. It's your home. I'm not… I mean…"

She flaps her arms and I chuckle. She's adorable when she's flustered.

I stalk to her and palm her neck. "This is your home, too. I want you with me wherever I am."

She blows out a breath. "Okay, but we're not living together or anything."

I kiss her nose. "Love you, Bunny. Now go before you're late."

I spin her around and pat her ass to get her moving. She yelps before rushing down the porch steps to her car.

I watch her drive off. The driveway is as bumpy as ever. I need to get it fixed. Although, I won't be living here forever. As soon as my injury is healed, I'll be gone again.

I frown. I need to discuss the future with Maya, but I'm worried about her reaction. She's going to be upset when she finds out I plan to return to active duty. She admitted she worried about me when I was gone, and I hate for her to worry. But I'm a soldier. It's the only thing I know how to be.

I force thoughts of the future away. They're a problem for another day.

I make my way to the backyard to chop wood for the fireplace. I grab the axe and get to work. It isn't long before my arms, shoulders, and upper back are aching from the workout.

I need to get back to the gym and work on my upper body strength. My core and leg muscles are getting worked plenty at physical therapy, but I've been neglecting the other muscle groups.

Despite the cool wind blowing off the Atlantic Ocean, I'm sweating up a storm. I stop to remove my flannel shirt.

"Caleb!"

I glance over my shoulder to discover Hudson leaning against the cabin.

"Are you watching me chop wood?"

He chuckles. "I've learned it's better not to interrupt a man working with an axe. Especially if he's former military."

I scowl. I'm not *former* military.

"You ready for a break? I have a proposition for you."

I grunt and march to the cabin. I open the door to allow him to enter first before following him inside.

"Coffee?"

"Sure," Hudson says as he scans the place. "Things have changed in here. It has a woman's touch now."

I frown at him. "Don't tell me you're here to gather gossip for Nova."

He holds up his hands. "Nah. Nova doesn't know I'm here."

"Sit." I motion to the kitchen table.

"What's this proposition?" I ask when I hand him his coffee.

He chuckles. "Going straight to the heart of the matter."

I shrug. What does he expect? Me to sit here and gossip about Smuggler's Hideaway? Not happening. And I'm certainly not telling him anything about my relationship with Maya. He was at drunk poker. He knows we're serious. There's nothing else to tell.

He sips on his coffee as he studies me. I wait him out. This isn't my first rodeo.

"I have a job for you."

I nearly startle. Of all the things I expected him to say, 'I have a job for you' didn't rank in the top hundred.

"A job?"

"You're aware I own *Hideaway Haven Resort*."

I nod. Everyone on the island knows he owns the resort. He built it after his career in the NFL came crashing to an end after an illegal tackle destroyed his ankle.

"Due to the kind of clientele we have, the resort has a decent amount of security."

"Makes sense."

The island is relatively safe but you can never be too safe. Especially when you're dealing with people who have money. They probably think nothing of leaving a ten-thousand-dollar diamond ring laying about and then cry thief when they misplace it.

"I'm currently recruiting a head of security."

"What happened to the former head of security?"

"He's tired of living on a tiny island where the choice in pussy is too limited." I grunt. "His words. Not mine."

"And you're telling me this because?"

"I want to hire you as my new head of security."

I'm shaking my head before he can finish the sentence. "No thanks. I have a job."

"You do?" His brow wrinkles. "The smuggler's grapevine hasn't caught up with it yet."

"Probably because my work isn't on the island."

"Are you going to fill me in?"

"It's not a big surprise. I'm returning to active duty."

His eyes widen. "You are? What about?" He nods toward my leg.

"I'm waiting to be medically cleared."

"Huh." He sips on his coffee. "I'm surprised."

"I don't know why it's a surprise. Being a soldier is my career."

"No one on the island expects you to return to active duty."

I don't ask how he knows this. I don't need to. The smuggler's grapevine is fast and thorough.

"What does everyone think I'm doing here?"

"We think you're back to stay."

"Nah." I shake my head. "I have no interest in crawling back here a failure."

He cocks a brow and I swear.

"Shit. I didn't mean you returned to the island a failure. You didn't have a choice after that tackle."

"And you do have a choice after whatever happened to you?"

I growl. "I do. I'm working my ass off to recover from my injury. Once my physical therapist signs me off, I'm out of here."

"Does Maya know this?"

"Maya knows I'm a soldier," I hedge.

"But does she know you're planning to return to active duty?"

No, because I've been avoiding the conversation.

"Maya's a strong woman. If being a soldier is what you want, she'll support you."

Hope flares to life in my belly. I need him to be right. Because I can't lose Maya. I love her more than anything. But I can't live on this island as a failure either.

"Maya's the strongest woman I know."

He grins. "She's strong, but not as strong as my Nova."

I hold up my hands. "Not gonna fight you."

"Good." He stands. "The offer for head of security is there if you need it."

I scowl. "I'm good."

I walk with him to the door.

"And you don't need to chop wood. The resort supplies wood to all of our cottages."

"I enjoy the exercise."

He grins. "I figured as much, but thought I'd offer."

I watch as he hops into a golf cart and drives toward the resort.

I hope he's right. I hope Maya will support me once she finds out I want to return to active duty. She'll worry about me when I'm gone but I'll come home to her as often as I can. We can make it work.

And if we can't?

I force the thought away. I don't want to consider the possibility of losing Maya.

I know how it feels to live without her. I'm not going back.

Chapter 27

"You can't celebrate without moonshine. At least, not on Smuggler's Hideaway." ~ Maya

MAYA

I stand in the parking lot of *Five Fathoms Brewing* with Nova, Paisley, Sophia, and Chloe as we watch the representatives from *Gourmet Corner* drive away.

When they turn the corner and are out of sight, Sophia squeals. "Thank the mermaids in the sea!"

Chloe and her join hands and bounce up and down in the parking lot while giggling.

Nova sighs. "I'd join them but I'm too exhausted for jumping."

"Being a parent of an infant is difficult but you'll miss these days when they're gone," Paisley says.

Nova's smile is wistful. "You're probably right."

"We are going out to celebrate!" Sophia declares.

"There's nothing to celebrate yet," I caution. "We haven't made any sales yet."

"But we will," Nova says. "With our beer in every single store of *Gourmet Corner* – not just the East Coast – we will be making tons of sales."

"And I shall be brewing more beer," Paisley says. "We need to discuss expanding our brewing capabilities."

Chloe rolls her eyes. "Of course, Paisley is going to use this as an opportunity to get more brewing stuff."

"Brewing stuff?" Paisley pushes her glasses up her nose. "You do realize this business is a brewery?"

"Let's discuss this at *Rumrunner*." Sophia rubs her hands together. "I'm in the mood for a moonshine celebration."

I groan. Sophia in the mood for moonshine equals a hangover each and every time.

Chloe circles her hand in the air. "Get your shit, mermaids. It's time to par-tay!"

While they hustle upstairs to the offices, I phone Caleb.

"Hey, Caleb. Just wanted to let you know I'm going out with my girlfriends tonight."

He chuckles. "I'll alert the police."

"We're not *that* bad."

"Do I need to remind you of the time you pranked the principal and ended up locked in her office in a chicken suit?"

"It wasn't a chicken suit. I was an otter."

"Yes, we should concentrate on the costume you were wearing when you got caught."

"Whatever."

"Call me when you need me to pick you up."

"I can find a ride home."

He grunts. "Call me when you need me to come pick you up."

"Fine, soldier boy. I'll call you."

"Have fun. Love you." He hangs up before I have the chance to say the same. And here I was worried about love bombing him. Turns out Caleb is the expert at love bombing.

Sophia rushes out of the brewery with Chloe hot on her heels. "Come on. Let's go."

We walk to *Rumrunner* since it's not too far. The bar is a speakeasy complete with a hidden entrance in an alley. Tourists are required to get a password from their website but locals are admitted without one.

"Hey, Trent," Chloe greets when he opens the speakeasy window.

He opens the door and motions us in. "Try to be on your best behavior."

I duck my chin to hide my amusement. My friends on their best behavior? Not in this lifetime.

Sophia and Chloe march straight to the bar.

Nova threads her arm through mine. "This is going to be fun. I haven't been out since Iliana was born."

"Harper!" Sophia shouts and slaps her palm on the bar.

The owner of *Rumrunner* saunters her way. "Uh oh. Trouble has arrived."

"Five shots of moonshine, please."

"I hope you're celebrating today," Harper says as she pours our shots. "You tend to cause less destruction when you're celebrating as opposed to commiserating over someone's broken heart."

Sophia grins. "Don't you worry. We're celebrating. Because we are awesome."

Harper rolls her eyes as she hands out the shots. Sophia holds up her glass. "Here's to the bootleggers. Masters of the sneaky sips and secret stashes. Thanks for keeping the party alive."

We raise our glasses. "To the bootleggers."

I throw back the shot. The alcohol burns. Moonshine on Smuggler's Hideaway isn't similar to moonshine anywhere else. It's strong as hell, doesn't have any flavor, and is oddly addictive.

Chloe elbows Paisley and points to a man exiting the storeroom. "Isn't that Eli?"

Paisley growls at her. "I don't care if it is. Would you stop obsessing over him?"

She snorts. "Stop obsessing over a local boy we went to high school with who is now a billionaire? Not in this lifetime."

"Plus, he owns *Buccaneer's Whiskey & Distillery*," Sophia adds. "Our biggest competitor."

Paisley scowls. "We brew beer. A distillery is not our competition."

"It is Eli. Eli!" Chloe waves. "Over here!"

Eli glances over at us, and Paisley drops to her knees. He starts toward us, and Paisley crawls behind the bar. Harper raises an eyebrow at her, and Paisley places a finger over her mouth.

I scoot behind Nova. I'm fine interacting with my friends, but I haven't spoken to Eli since high school. He's practically a stranger. Nova pats my hip. She's got my back.

"What are you celebrating?" Eli asks in greeting.

Chloe puffs out her chest. "A deal with *Gourmet Corner*."

"Congrats." He nods to Harper. "Next round is on me."

Harper sighs. "They're going to pick the most expensive drink in the bar."

He chuckles. "I figured as much." He nods to Chloe and Sophia. "Good to see you."

I watch the door close behind him. Once the coast is clear, I kneel down in front of Paisley. "He's gone."

She frowns as she stands. "I don't know who you mean. I was searching for my phone."

"Behind my bar?" Harper asks.

Chloe points to Paisley's hand. "You're holding your phone."

Paisley's cheeks darken but she doesn't give up. "Yes. After I found it on the floor."

I open my mouth to comfort her – being teased about the man you can't have is no fun – but the door to the bar slams open and my parents saunter inside.

"Shit," Chloe mutters.

Nova tries to shove me behind her. "I've got this."

I shackle her wrist to stop her. "No. This is my problem. My responsibility."

She studies my face. "Are you sure?"

"I already messaged Caleb and I'm messaging Weston now," Sophia says.

I smile at her in thanks before inhaling a deep breath and making my way to my parents.

Mom sneers at me. "I heard you were making a fool of yourself."

Making a fool of myself? I'm having a drink to celebrate our business. How is—

Holy smugglers on the run! Everything suddenly makes sense. She's jealous. My mom is jealous of my success.

It's all becoming clear to me now. She's lashing out at me because I have the life she wishes she could have. She's my mother. She should be happy for me. But she never will be.

The truth of the statement hits me in my chest and I nearly stumble. Nova presses a hand on my lower back to keep me steady. I glance behind me. All of my girlfriends followed me and are now standing behind me. Surrounding me with their support.

Their support gives me the courage to speak my mind. "I'm not the one making a fool of herself."

"How dare you?" she screeches and I wince at the high tone.

"Maya," Dad grumbles. "Treat your mother with respect."

Respect? He doesn't know the meaning of the word. Where is his respect for Mom? Or me?

And just like that I'm done. I'm done trying to win their love. I'm done kowtowing to them. I'm just plain done.

I snort. "The way you treat her with respect?"

His eyes narrow and his nostrils flare. "Do not question me, Maya. I am your father."

"No, you're not. You were never a father to me. You never encouraged me, supported me, nurtured me. You never loved me."

Mom leans close to sneer at me. "Maybe because you're unlovable." This time I do stumble. The venom in her voice feels like acid in my stomach.

"I love Maya," Nova says.

"I do as well," Paisley adds.

"Me too," Sophia and Chloe say in unison.

Their love washes away the acid working its way through my stomach. I should have let my friends in more growing up. I should have leaned on them more. I can't fix the past but I can work to create a better present and future.

I shoo my parents toward the door. "You should go before Caleb shows up."

"Poor little Maya. She needs a man to save her," Mom taunts.

I chuckle. "Are you serious? I don't need a man to save me. I'm not the one who's clinging to a husband who abuses her. I have a man who loves me. Who cherishes me. Who would never in a million years hit me in anger."

Mom shakes her fist at me. "How dare you? How dare you tell lies to the town?"

Weston saunters our way. I didn't realize he'd arrived at the bar already. He hitches his thumbs in his duty belt and stares down my mom. "If anyone is lying, it's you. Not Maya."

Dad frowns. "Maybe we should go."

"Good idea." Weston nods. "Run away before Caleb arrives."

"This is ridiculous!" Mom stomps her foot. "I'm allowed to have a conversation with my own daughter."

My anger ignites. It's like a fire in my belly. The door flies open as Caleb arrives but I ignore him. I lean close to hiss at my mom.

"I am not your daughter. You were never a mother to me. Sophia's mom was my mother. She's the one who explained things when I got my period. She's the one I went to when the bullies started attacking me. She's the one who fought for me when I was wrongfully accused of cheating. She's the one I love."

"Lily always did think she was better than the rest of us on the island."

Caleb sidles up to me. "You're done. Leave now or I'll have Weston remove you."

"You can't have us removed," Dad sputters.

"I can," Harper pipes in. "The management reserves the right to refuse service to jackasses."

Weston removes his handcuffs from his belt and twirls them in the air. "What'll it be? Walk out of here on your own or I remove you? I know which option I prefer."

Dad grabs Mom's upper arm and steers her toward the door. "I'll be speaking to the mayor about this."

"I'll phone Lana and let her know to expect your call," Weston hollers after them.

The door shuts behind them and I collapse into Caleb's arms.

"You okay?"

I start to say I'm fine but stop to consider his question. To my surprise, I am okay. I'm not devastated my parents don't love me. Because I have the love of a whole bunch of people who deserve my loyalty. My parents do not.

Don't get me wrong. I'll probably have moments when I yearn for my parents' love all over again but I will work my ass off to ensure those moments remain moments. I'm done with the all-encompassing yearning I've been feeling for years.

"Yes." I smile up at him. "I'm okay."

"Proud of you, Bunny."

Tingles spread through my body until I'm vibrating with happiness. Having the man I love be proud of me is the best feeling ever.

A champagne cork pops behind me.

"We definitely have something to celebrate now!" Sophia shouts.

I giggle. My friends are the best.

Chapter 28

"Where's a fire alarm when you need one?" ~ *Maya*

MAYA

Caleb opens the truck door for me and grasps my waist to lift me down. I shiver. I love it when he demonstrates how strong he is. I can't wait for wall sex. Although, I haven't pushed him on it since I don't know the extent of the injuries on his leg.

I frown. He's still holding back on me.

"What's wrong?" He scans the area for threats.

"Nothing's wrong," I lie. "But I worry the restaurant will be too crowded for you."

He squeezes my hand. "I'm fine. I'm with you."

I love the idea of being his personal good luck charm. But I don't want him to have another panic attack. He's still embarrassed about the previous one. Which is dumb, but emotions aren't logical. Even smarty pants Paisley crawled on the floor when she saw Eli.

"Nevertheless, if it gets to be too much, remember our signal." I tug on my earlobe three times.

He chuckles. "You're a crazy bunny."

"Crazy bunnies are the best kind. We make people laugh. And we never get caught and eaten for Easter dinner."

He throws an arm over my shoulders and steers me inside. My mouth drops open when we enter the restaurant at the *Hideaway Haven Resort.*

"I can't believe you chose this place. It's fancy." My nose wrinkles. "And expensive."

He taps my nose. "Don't you worry. Hudson offered me a discount."

"Must be nice to know the owner."

He chuckles. "You know the owner, too."

"True. But I don't know if he still holds my spying on him in high school against me. It was on Nova's orders but still. He was not happy to see me when he opened his locker and I popped out."

Caleb gives his name to the hostess and she leads us to a table in the corner. It's next to the window with a view of the ocean.

"This knowing the owner stuff rocks," I say as I settle in my chair.

"I know the owner of this awesome brewery. The smuggler's grapevine claims they're the best thing since sliced bread."

My cheeks warm at his compliment. "I wouldn't say sliced bread but definitely since indoor plumbing."

"Does the resort carry your beer?"

I giggle. "They do now."

"Explain."

"Well," I say before telling the story of how Nova got knocked up with Hudson's child. "And now you know why *Five Fathoms* beer is sold here."

He chuckles. "They really got locked in a chalet overnight?"

I shrug. "According to the story but..." I scan the room to make sure no one is listening to us before leaning close and whispering, "How did Nova get away the next morning before the contractor showed up if they were locked in? I say Hudson fibbed because he finally had what he wanted."

Caleb's blue eyes darken. "I know how it feels to finally have what you wanted all along."

I wiggle in my seat. "Me too."

The waitress arrives and we order the chef's surprise special and a couple of beers. Once we're alone, Caleb stands. "I need the restroom. I'll be right back."

I watch as he strides across the restaurant. There's a slight hitch to his walk but he's still utter perfection to me. Those broad shoulders I know are strong enough to chop wood all morning. Those narrow hips I love to dig my fingers in when he's buried deep inside me. I fan my face as memories flash through my mind.

Once he's out of view, I dig my phone out of my purse and open a game. Being alone in a restaurant where other people can look at me makes me antsy. Better to bury my head in a game.

I finish the second round of my game and frown. Caleb's been gone for five minutes. Worry tries to worm itself through me but I ignore it. He probably bumped into Hudson and lost track of time.

Another five minutes pass and now I am officially worried. I send Caleb a message.

Our appetizers are here. Are you okay?

There. I don't sound like a complete worry wort. I press send and wait.

And wait.

Two minutes pass before he messages back.

No.

I jump to my feet and run out of the restaurant. I can feel people's eyes on me but I ignore them. My discomfort at being the center of attention is not what's important now.

When I reach the lobby, I scan the area. Where are the stupid restrooms? I know they're here. This isn't my first visit to the resort. Chloe got married here.

I finally spot the men's room and hurry to it. I rush inside.

"Caleb? Are you in here?"

"Here."

I lock the door behind me before searching the room. Shit. Caleb's lying on the floor. I help him to sit up.

"Can you stand?"

He scowls. "Let me try."

I lace my arm through his and help him to his feet. He's nearly standing when his left leg collapses. I try to take his weight but he's too heavy for me. He crumples to the floor and I barely manage not to fall with him.

I make sure he's settled against the wall. "Let me go get help."

"Hudson," he grits out. "No one else."

"No one else," I promise. I dial Hudson's number.

"Maya?" He answers. "I'll get Nova for you."

"No!" I clear my throat. "I need you. Men's restroom in the main resort building. As fast as possible."

"On my way."

"He'll be here in a few minutes," I tell Caleb although I don't know where Hudson is. "Meanwhile, I bet our appetizers are stone cold."

"I don't give a shit about our food."

"Sorry. Sorry. Sorry. I was trying to be funny. Note to self. Don't be funny when you're locked in the men's restroom with Caleb. He doesn't find it amusing."

I check the time on my phone. Thirty seconds have passed.

"Where is Hudson? No wonder he's no longer in the NFL. He's slow," I mutter.

Someone knocks on the door and I hurry to unlock it. Hudson pushes inside.

"Fuck," he swears under his breath when he notices Caleb leaning against the wall. "It's your left leg?" he asks and Caleb nods while I wring my hands.

"How can I help?"

Hudson hauls Caleb to his feet. "Get the door."

I rush to open it for them.

Hudson helps Caleb to the door. "Don't want anyone to see me."

"Don't worry, bro. My golf cart is parked near the emergency exit."

We enter the lobby. There are people everywhere. Was it this busy before? Caleb's sweating and he's gasping for breath. Oh no. Is he having a panic attack? Not on my watch.

"Wow!" I shout and point outside. "Someone's skinny dipping in the pool."

The crowd rushes toward the swimming pool while we sneak out the emergency exit.

Hudson situates Caleb in the front seat of the golf cart.

"Do you want me to drive your truck back?"

Caleb clutches my hand. "Stay with me."

"Of course. Whatever you want."

I sit on the back of the golfcart and Hudson drives us to the cabin. It's not far since the cabin is on the edge of the resort's property. When we arrive, Hudson helps Caleb inside and settles him on the sofa.

"Try icing the area and, if it's not too painful, massaging," Hudson says as he passes me on his way out the door.

"Thank you."

He nods and I close the door behind him.

I rush to the kitchen and open the freezer. My eyes bulge out when I notice it's full of ice packs. Caleb and I need to have a serious conversation about his injuries but not now. I grab an ice pack and a towel.

Caleb's mouth is bracketed with pain when I return to him. "Um." I glance down at his jeans. "I think this works better applied to the skin and not over clothing."

"Fuck," he mutters.

"Shall I go? I don't want to go. I want to stay here and take care of you but if you're uncomfortable with me being here, I'll go. I can call Hudson back. He's familiar with injuries."

Caleb grasps my hands and tugs until I'm sitting down next to him. "I don't want you to go but I'm afraid you'll want to."

"Why would I want to go anywhere? Do you have gas?" I wrinkle my nose.

He chuckles. "Only my bunny could make me laugh at a time like this."

I smile. "I love you. And I love making you smile. Your dimple comes out and your hotness level goes from ten to fifty."

"I hope you still love me after you see this." He unbuttons his pants.

"Pretty sure *that* has given me tons of orgasms. And, let's face it, the penis isn't the most beautiful sexual organ."

"Penis?" He snorts. "I figured with as many romance books as you read you would say cock."

"It's a cock when it's aroused. Otherwise, it's a penis."

He taps his zipper. "Are you ready for this?"

"Caleb, you could show me you have a tail and I wouldn't care. I love you."

Whatever it is. However bad it is. I will stand by Caleb. That's how love works.

Chapter 29

"It's been Maya all along." ~ Caleb

CALEB

Maya's words of love give me the extra boost of confidence I need to push down my zipper. I lift up my ass and she helps to draw my jeans down my legs.

I can't look at her face. I don't want to watch the disgust form there when she realizes how badly injured my leg was. When she sees the mottled skin, the scorched area where the bullet exited my thigh, the jagged edges around the bullet hole.

"Who did this to you?" She growls.

Growls? I slowly swivel my head to catch her gaze. There's no disgust there. She's angry. No, not angry. She's pissed.

"Those mo-fos."

I chuckle. "Mo-fos?"

"Mother f-ers. I hope you busted a cap in their ass after this."

Laughter bursts out of me. "Busted a cap in their ass? Am I gangster now?"

"Do not make fun of me. This is not a funny situation."

I sober. "You're right. It's not."

"What happened?"

"I can't tell you." I'm a coward. I'm hiding behind operational security. But I don't want to tell the woman I love how I failed. How I caused a fellow soldier to lose his leg. Guilt swamps me but Maya huffs and I focus on her.

"I know you can't tell me where you were or who you were fighting. We've been pen pals for over a decade. I know the drill. I'm not an idiot. But you can tell me the broad strokes." She caresses my thigh. "How did this happen?"

"I was trying to escape with my squad when I was shot by an AK-47. The bullet hit me in the back of my thigh and exited in the front."

She gasps. "Sounds painful."

The worst pain in my fucking life. "The bullet shattered my femur and tore my muscles all to hell."

"Wow. I can't believe you can walk."

I grunt. "Didn't walk tonight, did I?"

"Stop the smugglers! You're in pain. I'm a selfish cow. I forgot."

She lays the ice pack on my thigh and pain shoots through my leg. I grit my teeth to stop myself from groaning.

"Do you have any pain medication?"

"The stuff the hospital gave me makes me groggy."

"What about over-the-counter pain meds? Do they help?"

I debate lying and saying I don't need anything. But if I don't take at least the edge off of this pain, I won't make it to the bedroom on my own. It wouldn't be the first time I slept on the sofa. But I can't sleep on the sofa with Maya here for the night.

I point to the kitchen. "I have some Tylenol in the drawer next to the refrigerator."

Maya jumps up and rushes to the kitchen. She returns seconds later with two pills and a glass of water.

"Now," she says once I've swallowed the pills. "Hudson said I should massage the area. What do you think? Will a massage help?"

Despite the pain rushing through my leg, my cock twitches at her question. My cock might be on board with a massage but I'm not. It's bad enough Maya saw my injury. She doesn't need to touch it. Her skin is smooth and soft. My thigh feels rough and hard. It's the opposite of sexy.

She narrows her eyes on me. "Are you being all weird again?"

"Weird?"

She motions to my leg. "You've been secretive about your injury since you came home."

"Hell yeah, I have. Look at it. You're gorgeous and I'm a certified freak."

"You're lucky I don't believe in violence," she grumbles. "Or I'd slap you."

I rear back. "Slap me? You'd slap me?"

"Slap some sense into you. How dare you call yourself a freak! You're not a freak. You're a hero. You're my hero."

I'm not a hero. If she knew what really happened, she'd realize the truth. And then she'd dump my ass. Which is why she's never finding out the truth.

"I'm nobody's hero."

"Agree to disagree. Now, do you want a massage or do you want to continue to be a big baby?"

"Are you saying I'm a baby?"

"I didn't stutter, did I?"

"What happened to my shy, sweet Maya?"

She purses her lips. "Why does everyone think being shy means I'm meek? There's a difference between the two, you know."

I hold up my hands. "Sorry, I questioned you."

She pokes me in the chest. "You should be sorry. You know better than to think I'm meek. And I'm not shy when I'm with you. You make me feel safe. Safe enough to be myself without worrying about what other people think."

Warmth spreads through my chest at her words. Despite everything – how I pushed her away for a decade, how I treated her when I first came home – she feels safe with me.

I hope I can live up to her expectations. I've failed my friends before. I can't fail Maya. I can't live without her. She's the one person I need to breathe.

I palm her neck and lay my forehead against hers. "I love you, Bunny."

"And I love you, soldier. But sometimes I want to kick you when you get all stubborn."

I chuckle. "I know another person who's extremely stubborn."

"It's not stubborn when I'm always right."

I rub my thumb over her pouty lips. "Always?" She nods. "Even when you got detention from the principal for setting off glitter bombs in the vice principal's office?"

She rolls her eyes. "It was a misunderstanding."

I cock an eyebrow. "You didn't set off glitter bombs in the vice principal's office?"

"I plead the fifth."

Pain shoots through my thigh and I grunt.

Maya frowns. "What is it? More pain? The ice isn't working. Shall I try to massage the area?"

I open my mouth to tell her fuck no but she holds up a hand. "Sorry. That sounded like a question. It wasn't."

She stands before dropping to her knees between my legs. My cock twitches with such vehemence it nearly escapes my underwear.

"First, let's get rid of any impediments." She shimmies my jeans down my legs until the material is pooled around my boots.

"I'm beginning to think romance books are big, fat liars," she mutters as she unties my boots. "I swear no one ever has problems with shoes or boots in the sexy scenes. What happens to their footwear? Does it magically disappear?"

She lifts my foot and yanks off my left boot. "I guess they could magically disappear in a paranormal romance. Vampires have lots of magical powers, too."

She rids me of my other boot before pulling my jeans off of me.

"There. Much better."

"You needed me without pants to give my thigh a massage?"

She points at my face. "You're smiling and your dimple is out. I'm winning."

She pushes my knees apart and scoots in between them. My cock hardens and lengthens at the sight. "Pretty sure I'm winning."

"This is just a massage. It's not foreplay."

"Bunny, you have your hands on my naked skin. My cock doesn't care if you're giving me a massage or not."

Her gaze drops to my cock and she licks her lips. I groan. "You're not helping the situation."

She bats her eyelashes at me. "What situation?"

"Vixen," I mutter.

She giggles. "I don't think muttering vixen is the deterrent you think it is. I've always wanted to be a vixen. The sexy heroine in my own story."

I thread a hand through her hair. "Maya, you are the sexy heroine in your own story."

She rolls her eyes and I tug on her hair. "Look at where you are."

"I'm about to give you a massage."

"No, Bunny. Look at where you are. You're in this cabin with me with my pants down and my injury on full display. When I returned home a few months ago, I was determined to become a hermit. I didn't plan to leave the cabin except for physical therapy."

"But you came to Nova's baby shower."

"Because I couldn't help myself. I knew you'd be there and I wanted to see you. Just once to get my fix. I told myself once would be enough."

"Until I badgered you to let me in."

I grunt. "You stopped by a grand total of three times before my resistance crumbled."

"Because your parents showed up."

"Do you know how many times they showed up and I refused to let them in? More than a dozen."

She gasps. "And you didn't let them in?"

"Are you starting to understand the influence you have on me now?"

She nods to my hard cock. "I think I understand a bit of the influence."

"Don't get me wrong. I want to bury myself inside you until I don't know where you start and I end, but it's more than sex. You, Maya Jenkins, are my everything. You have no idea how I lived for your letters and care packages. How your funny stories and sweetness kept me going all these years."

"It's always been you, Maya. From the first time, I chased those bullies away and you stared at me with those whiskey eyes, you ensnared me."

Her lips tremble and her eyes swell. "You ensnared me, too."

"Good." I nod. "Because you are never getting rid of me."

"I'm never letting you go."

I lean over to kiss her but she scoots away. "Nope. No kissing." She waggles her eyebrows. "On the mouth."

"You don't have to—"

My words are cut off when she slips her hand into my briefs and wraps it around my cock. She pumps up and down a few times before opening her mouth and taking me inside.

"Fuck," I groan as my cock is surrounded by her warm mouth.

My thigh trembles with pain but I ignore it. I can handle all the pain in the world to feel Maya's mouth around my cock.

Chapter 30

"Don't pity me." ~ Caleb

CALEB

"What's up with you today?" Hazel asks during our physical therapy session the next day. "You're a grumpy bear."

I grunt before I begin another round of squats. "You call me a grumpy bear every time we have a session."

"You're worse than normal."

I finish the squats and wipe the sweat from my brow before answering. "Bad day yesterday."

Her cheeks darken before she glances away. "What happened?"

"Are you fucking kidding me? Does everyone know?"

She widens her eyes and feigns confusion. "Know what?"

"Don't lie to me. You suck at it."

She rolls her eyes. "And you have ways to make me talk," she says in the worst imitation of a Russian accent ever.

"Hazel," I grumble.

"Fine," she huffs. "There might be a rumor floating around the smuggler's grapevine about an incident you had yesterday at *Hideaway Haven Resort.*"

"Fuck! I don't want the entire island to pity me."

She rears back. "Pity you? No one pities you."

I snort. "Sure, they don't. And no one spreads rumors behind my back either."

This gossipmongering island. I planned to return a man worthy of Maya. Instead, I'm pitied by the smugglers for constantly embarrassing myself.

Hazel points to the low platform. "Thirty seconds."

The smugglers may pity me but I don't have time for a pity party. I begin stepping up and down the platform. My left thigh protests every movement but I refuse to slow down. I am not letting this injury stop me. I refuse to be the cripple everyone points to at the grocery store.

"Time," Hazel calls.

I do one more step down. My left leg wobbles. I switch my weight to my right leg but it's tired from the workout and can't support me. I stumble and start to fall but Hazel catches me and helps me to sit down.

Fuck. It's been months since I got injured. I shouldn't be nearly collapsing from some step-ups. I growl. "I'm never going to get back on active duty if this doesn't improve."

Hazel's mouth gapes open. "Active duty?"

"What the hell do you think I'm doing here?"

"Physical therapy to recover from an injury."

"And once I'm recovered enough, I'll go in front of the medical evaluation board to get reinstated to active duty."

"You're serious?"

"What do you think? My life is a fucking joke?"

She holds up her hands. "I know it's not." She blows out a breath before dragging a chair over and sitting across from me.

"I thought the Army already honorably discharged you."

I shake my head. "Nope."

"But you're not in a medical retention processing unit." An MRPU is where soldiers usually recover from their injuries. But most civilians don't know what an MRPU is. I raise my eyebrow and she explains. "I did my internship at an MRPU."

"I managed to convince my commanding officer to give me convalescent leave. The leave is up soon and then I plan to go through the Medical Evaluation Board."

Hazel drops her chin to study the floor. I recognize the stalling tactic.

"What is it?"

"I'm not an expert. But when I interned at the MRPU, I had a few of my patients go through the Medical Evaluation Board and Physical Evaluation Board."

"And?" I push when she doesn't continue.

"It's not easy to get reinstated."

"I know. It's why I'm working my ass off."

She frowns. "You're pushing yourself too hard. Why do you think you had to be carried out of *Hideaway Haven Resort* yesterday?"

I growl. "I wasn't carried."

"Sorry. I shouldn't have said anything."

"No. Continue. You obviously have more to say."

She swallows. "Um…none of my soldiers returned to active duty."

"None?"

"Correction. Some returned to duty but they had modified duties or were reassigned under COAD."

"I don't qualify for continuation on active duty. I don't have fifteen years of active-duty service."

"Maybe I'm wrong. Maybe you'll sail through the medical board."

I glare at her. "Don't humor me. You nearly dislocated your jaw gaping when I said I want to return to active duty."

She drums her fingers on her thighs before asking, "Do you want my professional opinion?"

"I'm paying you to be a professional, aren't I?"

She hesitates for such a long time I figure she won't tell me her opinion. But she finally blows out a breath and speaks.

"It's my professional opinion that you are not medically fit to return to active duty. You've made vast improvements since we started working together but I don't think you will ever pass the physical army readiness tests."

My stomach spasms and I worry I'm going to throw up all over the floor.

"You're serious?"

"As serious as the asshole who shot you from behind."

"FUCK!" I stand and throw the chair across the room.

I can't believe this. My whole world is crashing down. Just when I thought I had everything I ever wanted. Everything I've longed for all these years.

Maybe Maya's dad was correct all those years ago when he said I'd never be man enough for Maya.

Chapter 31

"You want to play passive aggressive with me? Go ahead and try. I have years of experience." ~ Maya

MAYA

I frown down at my phone. I haven't heard from Caleb all day. I know he had physical therapy today, but he should have been home hours ago.

I tap my fingers on my steering wheel. What to do? Go home and hope Caleb's okay? Drive to the cabin and hope Caleb isn't mad at me for showing up unannounced? Neither choice is very appealing.

He loves you. Why would he be mad?

I start to ignore my inner voice but then force myself to woman up. Caleb does love me. He tells me often enough.

My parents are the assholes. They're the ones who are unlovable. Not me. Caleb loves me. My friends love me. Lily loves me. I am loveable.

I blow out a breath and switch on the engine to go check on Caleb. Nothing can be as bad as yesterday when he collapsed.

When I arrive at the cabin, it's dark. It appears abandoned, but Caleb's truck is here. Maybe he went to the resort to visit Hudson. I'll check.

"Caleb!" I call and knock on the door.

"Go away!"

Strangle a smuggler. Are we back to this? Does he regret showing me his injury yesterday?

I start to inch backwards. No. I stop myself. I'm the heroine in my own story and I won't be one of those wimpy heroines who make me want to throw my Kindle across the room. I will be strong. And fierce.

Maybe not fierce. But I can do strong.

"I wouldn't leave you alone before you said you loved me. What makes you think I will now?"

"FUCK! I don't want to see you."

"Too bad," I say and march inside the cabin.

I need to stop after a few steps since it's dark as midnight on the ocean with no stars in here. I let my eyes adjust but it's no use. It's too dark to see.

I creep to the wall and flip the switch. The lights flash on.

"What the hell? Lights are off for a reason," Caleb growls from where he's laying on the sofa with a bottle of moonshine in his hand. Potato chip bags are scattered on the coffee table along with an open pizza box with one piece of pizza left in it.

"What's going on?"

He sips from the bottle but doesn't answer me.

"Caleb," I plea. "What's going on?"

"Don't want to talk."

I drop my purse and shrug out of my coat before marching to the couch. I pick up the potato chip bags and the pizza box and carry them to the kitchen. I return with a glass of water and a cloth to clean the table.

"Here." I shove the glass into Caleb's hands. "If you don't want a hangover, drink this."

"Don't give a shit if I have a hangover. My life is over."

"Your life is over? What happened?"

"Some asshole shot the shit out of my leg while I was trying to escape with my squad."

I drop the cleaning supplies and plop down on the sofa across from Caleb. "This is not new information. Why is your life over now?"

"My days of being a soldier are done."

I'm confused. Is this news to him? He's lucky he survived his injury. A few inches to the left and the bullet would have hit his femoral artery. He would have bled out.

It's possible I spent way too much time obsessing over and googling bullet wounds today. I'm probably on some Internet watchlist now.

"I thought you were retired."

"I'm not retired. I'm on convalescent leave."

He is? I'm starting to realize I don't know Caleb's situation as well as I should. Why am I surprised? He wouldn't tell me about his injury until yesterday. He literally said I love you before he allowed me to see his leg.

"And you're going back to active duty?"

"Are you not fucking listening to me? I can't go back on active duty."

I flinch at his angry tone. Caleb can lose his temper but he's never been nasty to me before.

He takes another swig from the moonshine. The bottle is half empty. Did he drink half the bottle? This is not a good sign. Caleb isn't a drinker. A beer here and there but nothing more. Usually.

"Why can't you go back on active duty?"

"I told you. Some asshole shot me."

I inhale a deep breath before I lash out at him. One of us being angry is enough.

"Before today, you thought you were going back on active duty. What happened today?"

"I realized I'm a fucking cripple who will never pass the Army medical board."

"You're not a cripple."

He sneers at me. "Did you miss me sprawled out on the floor of the restroom yesterday?"

"It was a setback. There are always setbacks when you're recovering from an injury."

"Oh yeah?" He sips from the bottle. "What do you know about it?"

I start to tell him how I've been researching injuries but he continues before I have the chance.

"You're just a little mouse who's never gone anywhere and done anything. You've probably never traveled outside of the U.S."

As a matter of fact, I've been to Mexico for spring break but I don't answer him. He's on a tirade now. I know better than to interrupt someone mid tirade.

"You have no idea what it's like to face an enemy. To not know if you're going to live to fight another day. To watch people die. To lose friends, brothers really. You have no idea."

"No, I don't."

He sneers at me. "You don't even know what danger feels like. You think a few bullies cornering you is danger." He snorts. "So naïve."

And now I'm done. I no longer put up with men who take their anger out on me. Ironically, it was Caleb who taught me that.

I stand. "I'm leaving."

He shoos me toward the door. "Run away, little mouse. The adults are speaking now."

My nostrils flare as anger builds in my chest. But I keep my mouth clamped shut. This isn't my Caleb. The man I fell in love with. He's lashing out because he doesn't know how to handle his emotions.

"I'll speak to you later." After he's had some time to process the news. And no longer feels the need to lash out.

"I can't believe you're fucking leaving me. After all the pushing and pushing you did, you're leaving."

Oh goodie. We've reached the passive aggressive portion of our evening. I'm opting out.

"I am not leaving you. I'm leaving for the moment."

"Running away when you realize how hard it is to be with me? Typical."

He's starting to slur his words now. It won't be long before he's full on drunk. How he isn't full on drunk now is beyond me. A few swigs of moonshine and I'm ready to jump into the ocean and fulfill all of my mermaid fantasies.

"I'm not running away."

"You're at the door. That's the definition of running away." He points to the door and nearly falls off the sofa.

Whatever patience I still had disappears. I'm done with him blaming me for the situation. It's not my fault.

"No. Running away is when you listen to some asshole who tells you you're not a man."

He throws the bottle of moonshine across the room. It hits the wall and smashes into a million pieces. I lock my limbs before I rush to clean up the mess. This is not my mess to clean up.

"I'm not a fucking man. I'm a cripple."

"Can you stop using the word cripple?"

"Why?" He sneers. "Does it bother you that you love a cripple? Or maybe you're faking loving me because you pity me?"

"I'm not faking it. I love you, Caleb. I just don't like you very much at the moment."

"At the moment?" He opens his arms wide. "This is who I am."

"No, this is you lashing out because you got some bad news today."

"Bad news? My entire life is falling apart. It's more than bad news."

"Okay," I concede. "You received devastating news today. But you'll figure things out. This is a bump in the road. It's not the end of the road."

He slams his fist on his chest. "This is my road. I decide whether it's a bump or the end."

I need to leave. This discussion is not getting us anywhere.

"I'll call you later."

"Bye, bye, little mouse."

I flinch at his use of the nickname my bullies used but I don't say a word. It's a waste of breath. He's not listening to me.

I grab my bag and coat and open the door.

"I told you," he hollers after me. "Everyone in my life is better off without me."

No, we're not.

You're not getting rid of me, Caleb. Not ever. But I need some time and space to figure out how to deal with this new version of the man I love.

I pray to the mermaids this new version isn't permanent.

Chapter 32

"I didn't steal the moonshine." ~ Maya

MAYA

"Enough!" Nova yells.

What's going on? Why is Nova yelling? Nova is not a yeller. She's Ms. Sunshine on a Rainy Day.

I glance up from my computer to discover Chloe, Sophia, and Paisley are standing in front of my desk with Nova. My brow wrinkles. Chloe should be downstairs managing the restaurant and bar while Paisley should be across the parking lot in the brewery working on whatever she works on when she's there.

"What is everyone doing here?"

Nova grins. "We're here to cheer you up."

"And to save your fingernails." Nova points to my hand where I have indeed chewed off most of my fingernails.

"Her fingernails are a lost cause," Paisley observes.

I stuff my hands in my pockets. "Why are we discussing my fingernails?"

"Because Nova and Paisley are too nice to ask *why* you're chewing your fingernails," Sophia says. "I'm not. Why are you chewing your fingernails?"

I study her. "I get the distinct feeling you already know."

Which makes no sense. How could they possibly know what happened last evening with Caleb? I know the smuggler's grapevine is better than any spy network during the Cold War but we were inside a cabin in the woods. No one could have overheard us or happened to walk by.

"I don't have any details but you're obviously upset about something that happened with Caleb," Sophia says.

"Why do you think I'm upset with Caleb?"

She snorts. "Because every other morning you've flitted inside the office happy as a smuggler who fooled the police into thinking he was innocent."

"It's true." Chloe nods. "You've been happy as a mermaid who lured a sailor to his death."

Paisley sighs. "We've discussed this. Mermaids don't lure sailors to their death. And mermaids aren't real."

Chloe shoves her palm in Paisley's face. "Mermaids are real. End of discussion."

"I guess if you say the discussion is over, it is," Paisley mutters under her breath.

"You have two choices," Sophia announces. "You can tell us what happened here and now."

Not happening.

"What's my other choice?"

"We'll get you drunk at Mermaid Karaoke and then you'll spill all of your problems without us asking."

I hate to admit it, but Sophia's right. I am a bit of a blabbermouth when I've been downing shots of moonshine. But, really, who isn't?

Paisley's lips purse. "No one mentioned Mermaid Karaoke."

Chloe throws her arm over Paisley's shoulders. "You can handle a bit of Mermaid Karaoke for one night. It's to help Maya."

Paisley pushes Chloe's arm off of her. "Mermaids don't exist and karaoke is an excuse for people who think they can sing to be on a stage."

"I guess we're lucky Maya can sing then, aren't we?"

I bury my face in my hands. Why, oh why, did I ever join the choir in high school? Stupid Chloe and her stupid dares.

"Come on," Nova urges. "You aren't getting out of this. You can either embrace the suck or fight it, but it's happening."

"The suck?" Chloe scowls. "There's nothing sucky about the five of us going out together. We don't do it often enough anymore."

"Probably because the four of you fell in love and no longer have time to play drunk mermaid midget golf," Paisley points out.

"The question is – did Maya fall in love with Caleb?" Sophia asks.

Chloe snorts. "Is this a serious question? Maya's been in love with Caleb since she tutored him in math in high school. Although, I don't know how much tutoring happened since

Maya spent the entire time in the library staring at Caleb with cartoon hearts in her eyes."

"Fine." I push to my feet. "I will go to Mermaid Karaoke if everyone will just shut up."

Sophia bursts out laughing. "You're cute. You think we'll shut up."

Nova laces her arm through mine. "It'll be fun. I promise."

The *Bootlegger* is packed when we arrive. I scan the bar and groan. It's full of women dressed up as mermaids and men trying to catch them. In other words, it's my version of hell.

A man stops in front of us. "Hey, pretty lady, why aren't you dressed up as a mermaid? I bet your tits look fantastic in a bra top."

My cheeks warm and I drop my chin to stare at the floor.

Nova pulls on my arm. "She's taken."

"She's not wearing a ring. And what man would let his woman come to the bar on Mermaid Karaoke night without him?"

Chloe flashes her left hand in his face. "My husband doesn't let me do anything. I'm my own woman."

The man groans. "Feminists," he mutters before walking away.

"I knew this ring would come in handy."

Sophia giggles. "You flash your ring at every man who comes within five feet of you."

"It's pretty. Everyone should have the chance to enjoy it sparkle."

Sophia leads us to a booth in the corner with a reserved sign on it. She snatches the sign and stuffs it into her purse before sitting down. Paisley sits next to her, and Nova and I scoot into the seat across from them.

"Here." Chloe sets five shots of moonshine down on the table.

"How did you manage to order those in two minutes?" Paisley asks.

Chloe shrugs as she hands out the shots. "Here's to the—

"Someone stole my drinks!" A woman shouts behind Chloe.

"Quick. Drink up," Chloe urges.

"Are you trying to get into a barfight?" Sophia asks.

Chloe shrugs. "She's a mermaid. She won't fight me. I'm a smuggler."

"I think you mean thief," Paisley mutters.

Nova holds up her drink. "Here's to the bootleggers. Masters of sneaky sips and secret stashes. Thanks for keeping the party alive."

"To the bootleggers!" we shout as we lift our glasses and down the shots.

"Here," the bartender arrives and slams a bottle of moonshine on the table. "This ought to keep you from stealing other people's drinks for at least an hour."

"Thanks, Sloane."

She wags her finger at us. "No dancing on the tables, no stripping off your clothes, no getting into fights."

Sophia bats her eyelashes at Sloane. "We're on our best behavior."

Sloane snorts. "Your best behavior caused you to lead a strike against the science department in high school."

"Because you told me I wasn't allowed to slap the biology teacher."

"Why did you want to slap the biology teacher anyway?"

Sophia growls. "He told me I was only on the honor roll because my dad was a millionaire and he was buying my grades."

"But everyone knows you cheated on the biology test. You didn't buy your grades," Chloe says.

Sloane throws her arms up in the air. "And I'm out. Don't make me phone your brother to come arrest you."

"Joke's on you," Sophia hollers after her. "Weston isn't on duty tonight."

Chloe pours another round of shots. "How many of these do you have to drink before you tell us what fish crawled up your ass?"

"Two more," I say.

She slides two more shot glasses toward me. "Bottoms up."

I balk. "I was joking."

"I wasn't. As you very well know."

It's true. Chloe doesn't joke about drinking or confessions.

"Arrest a smuggler," I mutter before downing the first shot. Chloe nudges the second glass closer toward me. I glare at her as I pick it up. "Happy?" I ask when I finish it. She slides the next shot glass closer. I narrow my eyes and throw daggers at her as I drink it.

"Now." She rubs her hands together. "Tell us what happened."

Nova elbows me. "We're worried about you, Maya."

Ugh. She's bringing out the big guns. I don't want Nova worrying about me. She worries too much as it is. She's over her hypochondria but she still worries.

I motion to Chloe to pour me another shot. I'm already feeling warm and a bit woozy from the earlier shots but I need some additional courage before I pour my heart out to my friends.

"Caleb and I had a fight last night," I say when I finish the shot.

"About what?" Sophia asks.

"Cone of mermaid silence?" I wait for everyone to nod before continuing. "He found out yesterday that he can't return to active duty."

"He's far too injured to return to active duty," Paisley says.

"That's what I thought." I point to her but I don't know which Paisley to point to since there are now two of her.

"His injury is bad. I didn't realize how bad until he collapsed at the resort." I gasp and slam a hand over my mouth. I wasn't supposed to tell anyone.

Nova pries my hand away. "We already know about what happened."

"Promise not to say anything to Caleb. He's embarrassed. He thinks his injury makes him less of a man."

"How ridiculous." Paisley shakes her head. "A man is not judged by his physical prowess."

"How do you know how a man is judged?" Eli asks from behind her and she startles.

She glances over her shoulder at him. "You are not part of this conversation."

"I can't help but overhear when you're speaking at such a loud volume."

She motions with her hand for him to leave. "Go away. We don't want whatever you're selling."

"I'm not..." He scowls. "Whatever." He marches off and Paisley breathes a sigh of relief.

"Those two are going to be a riot," Chloe says.

Sophia slaps her shoulder. "One issue at a time."

"I'm not an issue. Caleb and I fought. He was an asshole. So, I left."

Nova's eyes widen. "You left?"

"I will not allow anyone to treat me the way he treated me."

She throws her arms around me. "I'm so proud of you."

"Let's drink shots to celebrate." Chloe pours another round of moonshine.

I down the shot. I'm starting to feel all fuzzy inside. I do love moonshine. And my friends. They're the best. I should probably tell them more often. I open my mouth to confess my love for them, but I'm cut off when someone announces my name.

"Maya Jenkins. You're up."

The woman on the stage waves the microphone at me while Nova hauls me out of the booth.

I glare at my so-called friends. "I'm going to kill you all in your sleep."

The music starts up and the first beats of *I Knew You Were Trouble* play.

I snatch the microphone. "I love this song!" I shout before I begin to sing.

I've known Caleb was trouble for nearly two decades. And yet I can't let him go. But I can't allow him to treat me the way he did yesterday. Plus, there's a good possibility he doesn't ever want to see me again after I walked away.

And here I thought I was getting my very own happily ever after. I should have known better.

I shove those thoughts out of my mind. My queen, Taylor, is singing. Never ignore your queen.

Caleb and our problems can wait. We've waited this long after all.

Chapter 33

"I really need to learn to lock my door." ~ Caleb

CALEB

I groan as I roll over in bed. My head protests the movement and my stomach gurgles. I'm afraid I'm going to throw up.

"There's a bucket next to the bed if you need to vomit," Hudson says.

Hudson? What the hell? Why is he here? I open my eyes and blink until the room comes into focus. Hudson isn't alone. Lucas and Flynn are with him. There's only one explanation for their presence.

"What did Maya tell you?"

Hudson growls. "She didn't tell us anything."

Ah, I guess there is another possible explanation. "What did your women tell you?"

"Nothing." Lucas frowns. "Which is very unusual for Chloe. I'm afraid she's going to burst soon."

Flynn nods. "Sophia didn't say anything either."

I force myself to sit up. If Maya didn't tell her friends what an asshole I was to her, who subsequently told their partners, then? "What are all of you doing here?"

Hudson crosses his arms over his chest. "We're not stupid."

I rub a hand over my forehead. My head is pounding and nothing is making any sense. "Never said you were."

He nods to the bedside table. "There are two pain pills."

"Thanks," I mutter before swallowing the pills with a bit of water.

"Our women went to Mermaid Karaoke yesterday," Flynn begins.

Maya and her friends at *Bootlegger* can only mean one thing. "How much bail money do they need?"

"Those women never pay bail money," Flynn says.

Lucas growls. "I won't allow Chloe to spend the night in jail."

Must be nice to be a cop.

"I have a special fund for bail money," Hudson says.

Or a millionaire.

"Can someone explain why you're here before my head explodes?" I ask.

"We're here because you hurt Maya. No one hurts Maya on our watch," Flynn says. "She's family."

I don't bother asking how they know I hurt Maya. Their circular talk makes my head hurt worse. "Maya deserves better than me."

"Better than a genuine American hero?" Hudson asks.

I scowl. "I'm not a hero."

There's a knock on the door and I moan. Who the hell is here now? When did my cabin in the woods become Grand Central Station? What does a man need to do to get a bit of peace on this island? Why did I stop locking my door?

"They're here," Hudson says. "Get dressed."

Lucas wrinkles his nose. "A shower wouldn't be a bad idea either."

Before I have a chance to protest, they leave the bedroom and shut the door behind them. I hear the front door open but as much as I strain to listen, I can't hear who it is. Is it Maya? Did she come back?

I need to see her. To apologize. I throw the covers off and get out of bed. I hurry to the bathroom and shower as fast as I can. I'm still putting on my t-shirt when I enter the living room. I screech to a halt.

"You're not Maya."

Kyle chuckles. "I've been accused of many things but a woman has never been one of them. Not even when I wore a hijab."

"What are you doing here?"

"I contacted him," Hudson says.

"How the hell do you even know who he is? Our missions are classified."

He shrugs. "I have contacts. A signed football greases a lot of palms."

I scowl at him. "Operational security isn't a joke."

He holds up his hands. "Never said it was. I didn't learn anything about your missions. Hell, I don't even know which countries you've served in. But when I reached out, I discovered Kyle was looking for you."

I face my former teammate. "Why the hell would you be looking for me?"

"Um... maybe because you cut yourself off from contact with everyone in the unit. Even the Cap wouldn't divulge your location while you're on convalescent leave."

"Convalescent leave is over," I snarl. "I'm being discharged."

"Fuck, bro. I'm sorry."

"Why the hell are you sorry? You should be glad I won't be returning to active duty where I can get other soldiers injured the way I got you injured."

Kyle's brow wrinkles. "What the hell are you talking about?"

"Do you need me to spell it out?" I motion toward his prosthetic leg. "You'd have a real one of those if it weren't for me."

He rears back. "Did you get hit on the head when those insurgents shot you in the leg? I'd be dead if it weren't for you."

"Don't lie."

He marches to me and I wince when I notice his limp from his prosthetic leg. He grasps my t-shirt and shakes me. "Enough of this pity party. It's not your fault I lost my leg."

"But if I had—"

He shakes me again. "Nope. I'm done listening to your idiotic lies. You couldn't have done anything differently. You don't have psychic abilities. You couldn't have anticipated there were twice as many insurgents in the building than our briefing indicated. You are not to blame for the actions of others. You hear me?"

I lift my hands. "I hear you."

He narrows his eyes. "But do you believe me?"

"I can slap some sense into him," Lucas offers.

"Slapping won't work." Hudson meets my gaze. "What does work is the help of a woman who loves you."

I snarl at him. "What do you know about it?"

Flynn barks out a laugh. "Hudson was nearly as much of a hermit before he got Nova pregnant as you were before you let Maya in."

"It's true." Hudson nods. "I was convinced my life was over because I couldn't play pro ball anymore. I thought I was a has-been who didn't deserve a woman like Nova."

"But you're a millionaire and own a successful business," I point out.

"You know as well as I do none of that shit matters if you think you're undeserving."

Kyle releases my t-shirt and throws an arm around my shoulder. "I approve of your new friends. They'll never be as good as me but they're damn close."

"The offer to be my head of security still stands," Hudson throws out. "In addition to the salary, the benefits include health insurance, free meals at the resort for you and your family, and living accommodations in a condo on the resort grounds."

"Dude." Kyle whistles. "Do you have any more job openings?"

"There's always room for a friend of Caleb's. Assuming you can convince Caleb to take the job."

"Challenge accepted."

I shove Kyle away. "Everyone needs to stop pushing me."

"Someone's got to push you, you knucklehead. Did this idiot ever tell you about the first time we went rappelling?" Kyle chuckles. "He cried like a baby."

"I didn't cry."

"But you wanted to." He grinds his knuckles over my head and I punch his shoulder. He laughs as he catches his balance on a chair.

"How do you do it?" I ask.

"Do what?"

"Laugh and joke when you lost part of yourself back there in the sandbox."

He sobers. "I didn't lose part of myself." I nod toward his leg. "My lower leg is a body part. It's not part of myself." He taps his fist on his chest. "In here. I'm still me."

"But your career is over."

"There are other careers."

"But you loved being in the Army."

"Not as much as I love my wife." He smiles. "She's happy as a pig in shit to have me home. She's pregnant."

"Mandy's pregnant?" He nods. "Congrats, bro."

"Thanks." He clears his throat. "And the Army is paying for my bachelor's degree. I'm going to be an engineer. Plus, I'm volunteering at the VA on weekends. Compared to some, I'm a lucky son of a bitch."

My throat tightens as guilt stabs me. I'm being a whiny bitch about my injury whereas Kyle lost part of his leg and he's moving on.

"You always were full of optimism."

"And you never shut up about the woman you were going to claim once you did your time in the Army." He scans the room. "Where is she? Did you finally man up?"

I scratch my neck. "I pushed Maya away."

"Dumbass," he mutters.

"It's why we're here," Lucas says. "We need to figure out a plan of action for him to win Maya back."

"I told you. Maya is better off without me."

"Dumbass," Kyle repeats. "We might need to get Mandy. She'll talk some sense into him."

"I can pick her up," Hudson volunteers.

"Whoa." I hold up my hands. "His wife is a ball buster."

Kyle grins. "She keeps me on the straight and narrow. Doesn't let me hold pity parties with a bottle of moonshine."

And the hits keep coming from him. I might as well confess now before they drag it out of me. "I might have said some nasty things to Maya after I found out I wasn't able to return to active duty."

"It sucks your Army career is over but you weren't planning to re-up in two years anyway," Kyle says.

I scowl. "But that was before…"

"Before what?" he asks. "Before you saved my life?"

"Stop saying I saved your life."

"Bro, I was bleeding out. You could have left me there. You were already in the clear. But you didn't. You came back and carried me out of there. You saved my life."

I frown. "You make me sound like a hero."

"Because you are." He slaps my back. "It takes time to adjust to civilian life. But you have a good group of friends to help you. And." He waggles his eyebrows. "If this Maya is as wonderful as you always claimed she was – and based on the chocolate chip cookies she used to send you every month, I think she is – she'll forgive you."

"All you need to do is cut your chest open and bleed for her," Flynn says.

I cringe. "Anyone else have a better plan?"

"Does she enjoy swimming?" Hudson asks. "I could put in a pool for you out back."

Lucas chuckles. "There's no way Maya is living in this cabin in the middle of nowhere."

Crap. Is he right? I don't want to live in town.

I shake my head. I'm making it all about me again. Which is how I landed in hot water to begin with. I need to start thinking about Maya. About the future without the Army. My heart stutters but I inhale a deep breath to calm myself.

I've survived worse than this. But I won't survive losing Maya. I don't want to.

Chapter 34

"Thanks for welcoming me to my own home." ~ Maya

MAYA

I frown as I walk toward my house. Caleb's truck is parked in the driveway. What is he doing here?

I haven't heard from him since the other night when he got drunk and mean. I've reached for my phone at least a million times to message him to ask if he's okay. But I managed to stop myself.

I am not going to be the lame heroine who lets the hero walk all over her. I hate those heroines. They drive me batty. I refuse to be her.

I realize I'm standing frozen in front of my house and force my legs to move forward. Despite my desire to be the strong heroine in my own story, I want to hear what Caleb has to say. Will he apologize or will he break my heart?

My heart spasms and I rub a hand over it. I'll be okay. Either way, I'll survive. I survived parents who don't love me. I can survive this.

I twist the knob but the door won't open. It must be bolted from the inside.

"Caleb!"

"Hold on. We're not ready."

"We? Who's we?"

If my girlfriends know what's happening and didn't tell me, I'll put yeast in their beers. Women should stick together.

I place my ear against the door but I don't hear any giggling or female voices. I do hear some grunting. What's going on?

I knock on the door. "Caleb, open this door this minute!"

Footsteps rush around the room before the backdoor opens and closes. The front door flies open and I nearly tip over. Caleb steadies me with a hand on my shoulder but I shrug him away. He has some apologizing to do before he's allowed to touch me again.

"What's going on? Why are you here?"

His arm sweeps toward the living room. "Come in."

What is he up to? I creep inside and scan the space. I gasp and drop my bag before rushing toward the corner of the room.

"What did you do?" I say as I run my hand along the bookshelves.

"I made you a reading nook."

And some reading nook it is! I've always struggled to figure out how to utilize this area. The real estate agent claimed it was a formal dining room but the round shape doesn't lend itself to a large dining table.

But now the walls are lined with bookshelves from floor to ceiling. There's also a comfy chair and footstool where I can spend hours reading. The book I'm currently reading sits on a cute little table next to the chair and there's a blanket folded on the footstool all ready for me to curl up under on a cold Winter's day.

"How did you manage to…"

My words trail off when I notice a picture frame in the middle of the books. I step closer. It's a picture of me from high school. I'm sitting in the library with a book open in front of me while smiling at the camera.

Caleb approaches until I can feel his warmth surrounding me. Until I can smell his earthy scent with its undertones of spice.

It's only been a few days but I've missed his smell. I've missed his warmth. I've missed laying with him in bed at night. I've missed him. Period.

He reaches past me to pick up the picture. "It's a little worn from use."

"From use?"

He smiles at the picture. "I carried this with me every single day I was away."

My heart stutters in my chest before my pulse quickens. "You did?"

"I thought I couldn't have you but I couldn't be without you either." He sets the picture back on the bookshelf.

All these years he's thought about me as much as I thought about him. I trace my bracelet with my finger. We both had mementos we couldn't let go.

He grasps my shoulders and spins me around to face him. "Will you forgive me, Bunny?"

I want to forgive him. I want to jump into his arms and taste his lips and forget all about the past week. But I'm not going to be the weak heroine. Not anymore.

"You can't just barge into my house and build me some bookshelves and expect me to forgive you."

"Full disclosure. I also moved my shit in."

My mouth drops open. He moved his stuff in? How dare he? I shove those thoughts away. One thing at a time.

"I know you were hurting, but the things you said to me..." I shake my head. "I deserve better." Caleb smiles and my brow furrows. "What are you smiling about?"

"Proud of you, Bunny. Proud of you finally realizing you deserve better."

I try to stop it but warmth fills me at his words. Nothing feels better than knowing the man you love is proud of you. I lean toward him but stop when I realize he hasn't apologized yet. Asking for forgiveness is not the same thing.

I scowl at him. "You can't say you're proud of me and everything is forgiven and forgotten."

"You're right. I'm sorry. I was an asshole. I should not have taken my anger out on you. It was unfair and wrong. I shouldn't have said the things I did." He hands me a card.

"What's this?"

He taps the card. "Read it."

It's the business card of a therapist. My mouth drops open. "You're going to therapy?"

"I still have a bumpy road ahead of me. I have a lot of guilt to deal with and I'm struggling with my time in the Army coming to an end before I was ready."

I appreciate him being open with me, but I have questions. "Why guilt?"

He grunts. "My buddy lost his leg because of me."

I don't know the situation. I don't know the buddy. But there's one thing I know for sure. "There's no way it's your fault."

He smiles at me and his eyes fill with wonder. "What did I do to deserve you?"

"Same, soldier boy."

He flinches. "I'm not a soldier anymore. It's official. I've been honorably discharged."

I squeeze his bicep. "I'm sorry, Caleb. I know being a soldier is important to you. But I'm certain you can figure out your next step. You need time is all."

"I already accepted a position with Hudson."

I rear back. "What?"

"I'm the new head of his security."

"Congratulations. You're going to rock at it."

He palms my cheeks. "Does this mean you forgive me?"

Of course, I forgive him. How could I not? The closed up hermit who initially refused to open his door to me admitted to his fears about the future and his guilt about the past. He's even starting therapy. Forgiveness granted.

"Yes." I smile up at him. "I forgive you."

"Thank fuck," he murmurs before his head descends.

I hold up a hand to stop his lips from meeting mine. My hand shakes, but I do it.

"We still haven't discussed you moving into my house."

Don't get me wrong. I want to live with him. But him moving in should be a decision we make together.

"Better to ask forgiveness than permission."

I stab him in the chest with my finger. "For future reference, this is not true."

"I'm sorry, Maya. I wanted to show you how serious I am. How sorry I am."

I bite my bottom lip. "But living in town? Will you be okay with having people around you all the time?"

"Smuggler's Rest isn't Kabul or Baghdad."

I guess I don't need to wonder what countries he's been stationed in any longer.

"Thank the mermaids it isn't."

"I know you prefer to be in town close to the brewery and *Bootlegger*."

He raises an eyebrow and my cheeks warm.

"What did you hear? I didn't wear a mermaid costume. That's an outright lie."

"But you did sing and declare Taylor Swift your queen and insist everyone in the bar bow down to her image on the screen?"

My cheeks are redder than the cranberries *Buccaneer's Distillery* puts in their gin by now.

"It's Chloe's fault. She stole moonshine shots from a mermaid."

"And then she forced the liquor down your throat."

"Yep. That's exactly what happened."

He chuckles. "I can't believe I ever thought I needed to escape Smuggler's Hideaway to find adventure."

I roll my eyes. "Silly you. Smuggler's Hideaway is the best. But don't think you're getting away with becoming a hermit on the island. I have places in the world I want to visit."

Places I've waited to visit until I could go with him.

He nods to the fantasy section of my library. "You do realize those places don't exist in the real world?"

"Really? Because they have maps and everything."

He groans. "You're going to force me to go on those trips where they recreate the book, aren't you?"

Duh. I've always wanted to visit New Zealand. Visit New Zealand and tour where the *Lord of the Rings* trilogy was filmed? It's a no brainer. It's also happening.

"Don't worry. You'll have fun."

He wraps his arms around me. "I'll have fun because I'm with you. We could be in the remotest spot on the planet and I'd have fun with you."

"Don't get any ideas. I'm not going on some cruise in the Arctic Circle to observe polar bears."

"You don't want to observe polar bears?"

"If you want to observe wildlife, visit Sammy the seal."

He chuckles and I enjoy the feel of his body moving against mine. This is where I belong. Not with my parents who don't love me and do everything in their power to make me miserable. But with Caleb. In his arms. Forever.

"I love you, Caleb."

"And I love you, Bunny."

His gaze drops to my mouth and I bite my bottom lip. He moans before his lips meld to mine. I open on a sigh. He growls as he plunges his tongue into my mouth. I press closer to him and—

"Knock! Knock!" Sophia shouts as she pounds on the door.

Caleb wrenches his lips from mine with a snarl.

"Why is Sophia at the door?"

"Shit. I forgot."

"Forgot what?"

"Your friends want to celebrate our relationship."

"But I've never had make-up sex before," I pout.

"You are not making this easy."

"I'm not the one who planned a party at the most inconvenient time ever."

"We better let them in before they barge inside." Caleb retreats a step before adjusting his cock.

I giggle. He deserves to be hard and horny. He's the one who planned the party.

He snatches my hand and leads me to the door. "You'll pay for that giggle."

"Promises. Promises," I taunt as I open the door and my friends pour into the house.

My cheeks ache from how big my smile is. I did it. I got everything I've ever wanted.

Chapter 35

"Next time I host a party there will be a password to gain entrance." ~ Caleb

CALEB

I scowl as Sophia, Chloe, Nova, and Paisley invade Maya's house with their partners and children. I start to shut the door after them.

"Hold on!" Lily shouts as she rushes up the porch with her husband, Jack. Weston and Scarlett are right behind them.

"Sorry, we're late," Scarlett apologizes. "Getting Weston out of the house on time is a chore."

Weston smirks. "If you weren't so sexy, I wouldn't have to attack you first."

"Hey, Sis!" Hazel hollers as she runs toward us. She greets Scarlett before smiling at me. "Sorry, I'm late."

"I didn't invite you."

She bursts into laughter. "You're cute. You think you can keep a party on Smuggler's Island small. We are smugglers!" She shakes her fist in the air.

Crap. How many people are coming to this party? It's supposed to be a small, intimate affair.

Maya clasps my hand and leans in close to whisper to me. "Are you okay?"

"Fine." I try to shut the door again but more people push their way inside.

"I can kick everyone out if you prefer."

I frown. "This party is supposed to be for you." She lifts an eyebrow and I quickly correct myself. "For us, I mean."

"Remember our signal if it gets to be too much." She tugs on her earlobe three times. "Or we could go hide out in the bedroom."

"No sneaking out on your own party," Chloe yells and I nearly jump. I should have better situational awareness but this large group of people has me off my game.

She places a hand on a young girl's shoulder. "This is my daughter, Natalia."

"Nice to meet you, Natalia."

She stares up at me. "Were you really in the Army?"

The past tense of her question nearly has me growling but I swallow it down. No matter how upsetting being discharged is, it's no excuse to growl at a child. Some day I hope the urge to growl when someone mentions my Army past is gone. But today is not that day.

"I was."

"Did you kill people?"

"Natalia!" Maya admonishes. "You can't ask him that."

"Why not? How am I supposed to decide if I want to enlist if I don't know?"

"You are not enlisting in the Army," Chloe orders.

"Why not? Is being a soldier not good enough?"

I cross my arms over my chest. "Yeah, Chloe. Is being a soldier not good enough for your daughter?"

Chloe squirms. "Lucas! Your daughter is misbehaving."

I was wrong. This party is fun after all.

Natalia rolls her eyes. "I'm *his* daughter whenever I do something you don't approve of."

"Duh. I only accept credit when I approve."

"I can't believe Chloe Summers – the wild child who devised a rappelling system to dive off the cliffs at *Mermaid Mystical Gardens* – has a child."

"I'm no longer wild." She narrows her eyes. "And you're not supposed to know about the rappelling system."

Lucas laughs as he joins us. "Chloe no longer wild? Sure. And you no longer phone in prank calls with the police either."

Chloe rolls her eyes. "Prank calls are childish. You need to fully commit to the prank before you alert the police."

Lucas snorts. "Like the time you released the parrot mascot from Pirate's Perch?"

Chloe gasps. "I would never release the mascot of another town on Smuggler's Rest."

"What about in high school when—"

She slaps a hand over my mouth. "Shush you. Don't make me add your name to my list of people who need to be pranked."

"And she's worried about me joining the Army," Natalia mutters.

Chloe squeezes Natalia's shoulders and steers her away. "Let's discuss this in private. Away from the military hero."

Lucas sighs as he follows them.

I throw an arm around Maya. "Your friends are crazy."

"They prefer the word unique."

"Naturally."

Nova arrives with a screaming Iliana in her arms. "I can't handle it anymore. Here." She shoves the baby toward me. "You handle her."

I retreat a step and hold up my hands. "What? Why?"

She doesn't give up. She pushes the baby against my chest and I don't have a choice but to catch her. She's tiny in my hands. I'm afraid I'm going to drop her. Then again, if I can manage not to drop a live grenade, I can handle this.

Iliana's mouth shuts and she stops screaming. She blinks up at me with bright blue eyes. They're gorgeous, but I would prefer a baby with whisky-colored eyes.

"He's getting baby fever. I told you this would work," Nova whispers to Maya.

I don't bother to look away from the baby when I ask, "What work?"

Maya runs her finger down Iliana's little nose. "Nova wants me to get pregnant so our children can grow up together."

The idea of Maya pregnant with my baby has my cock perking up. It's down with this idea. In fact, it's ready to kick everyone out of the house and begin working on the project immediately.

"How many children do you want?"

She stares at me with her mouth gaping open. "You're not running away."

"Why would I run away? I love you. We're living together. Next step is a baby."

"I think the next step is supposed to be marriage." Her eyes widen and she slaps a hand over her mouth. "Forget I said anything."

I chuckle. "You want to get married? We'll go down to the courthouse today."

"What if I want a big wedding with a white dress and twenty bridesmaids?"

I shrug. "Those bridesmaids will be walking down the aisle alone since I refuse to have twenty groomsmen but otherwise, I don't care. You want a wedding. You can have one."

Anything Maya wants, I will move mountains to give her. As long as I don't have to wear a baby blue tux, I'm all in.

"What if I want a romantic proposal?"

"Do you want a romantic proposal?"

Her cheeks darken but she nods.

"Then, I'll start googling how to perform a romantic proposal."

She giggles. "Or you could read for inspiration." She motions toward her reading nook.

I waggle my eyebrows. "I thought we'd use those books for another kind of inspiration."

"Enough." Nova pushes her way in between us. "I'm taking my baby back before the two of you teach her about sex."

"She's too young to understand sex," Lily says as she walks up to us with her husband, Jack, trailing her.

"I'm not chancing it." Nova steals Iliana from my arms. The baby starts to scream. "Dang it. My little girl is obsessed with men. This does not bode well for my future. Where's Hudson?" She wanders off.

"You appeared quite comfortable with a baby in your arms," Lily says once Nova is gone.

"Sweet flower," Jack grumbles from behind her. "Do not encourage them."

"Why not? I want more grandchildren."

He sighs. "I apologize for her."

I smile. "No need to apologize. My mother is the same."

"I'm the same what?" Mom says as she enters the house. My sisters and Dad follow her inside.

I tug on the collar of my t-shirt. It's getting crowded in here. These are my friends and family, I remind myself, but it doesn't help. I can feel the sweat gathering on my brow.

"Excuse us, Cora." Maya tags my hand and drags me through the crowd down the hallway to her bedroom.

I vaguely hear catcalls and laughter but they sound far away as if I'm underwater.

Once the door is shut behind us, Maya pushes me onto the bed. She stands between my legs and brushes her fingers through my hair.

"Shall we work on some breathing techniques?" I nod. "Deep breath in." I try to follow her instructions but I can't seem to get enough air. I choke and start coughing.

Maya rubs a hand up and down my back until the coughing subsides and I feel as if I can breathe again. "Better? Let's try again. Inhale a deep breath." This time I manage to inhale a breath without choking on air. "And let it out."

We go through the breathing exercises a few more times until my heart stops racing and my palms are no longer sweating.

I wrap my arms around Maya. "It shouldn't be this way. I know and care for every single person in this house. I shouldn't be panicking."

"And I shouldn't believe in vampires, but I do."

"I'm trying to be serious."

She pinches my chin. "Using logic to understand a panic attack will drive you crazy. There's nothing logical about panic attacks."

I drop my chin. "I embarrassed myself again."

She snorts. "Oh please. Everyone thinks we're in here having sex. There's nothing to be embarrassed about. Unless your performance is less than stellar."

I tickle her ribs. "I'll show you less than stellar."

"Please, don't!"

I smile up at her. "How do you do it?"

"Do what?"

"Bring me back and make me laugh."

"Silly man. Haven't you figured it out by now? You and I were meant for each other. If we were shifters – and don't you dare say shifters don't exist – we'd be fated mates."

"I've never been happier to have lied about not understanding the Pythagorean theory."

"Imagine all the things we could have done in the library if I hadn't needed to tutor you."

My cock twitches. It's down with whatever she wants to try. "The library is still around. We could try out some of your high school fantasies now."

"We might shock some of the local students."

I smirk. "I bet you know a few hiding spots."

"I—"

"Enough!" Paisley shouts loud enough for us to hear her.

"Uh oh," Maya mutters. "Paisley doesn't shout often but when she does… We better get out there."

She moves toward the door but stops. "Assuming you're okay. If not, we'll stay in here. I bet Natalia will sneak us some food and drink. She appeared enamored by you."

I stand. "I'm good. Let's go find out why Paisley's losing her mind."

"Are you ready?" She holds out her hand and I grasp it.

"Ready for the rest of my life with you."

She sighs. "You say the sweetest things."

"Only for you, Bunny. Only for you."

I'm not lying. Maya is the only person who I want to be sweet with. Although, once we have children, I'll be sweet with them, too.

Maybe I did lie.

Chapter 36

Paisley – a woman who's not always as cool, calm, and analytical as she appears

PAISLEY

I finish the pH test of the next batch of Summer Ale and check the time. Darn it. I'm late again. I clean up the lab as quickly as possible.

When I arrive at Maya's house, it's already crowded. I search for Maya and Caleb but I don't find them. I set my housewarming present next to the pile on the table and go in search of a beer.

"There you are," Sophia says when I enter the kitchen.

I start to push my glasses up my nose but fist my hand to stop myself. Pushing my glasses up my nose is a nervous habit. I realize this but I haven't been able to break the habit.

"Where else would I be?"

"In your lab."

"Someone has to actually make the beer for *Five Fathoms*. Otherwise, you would have nothing to market."

She sighs. "I didn't mean to offend you. But you work too hard. You need to get out more often."

And do what? It's not as if I have a loved one to spend time with. Or a family who I enjoy hanging out with. Plus, all of my friends are now partnered off and have less time for me.

Besides, I enjoy brewing beer. It's fun to think up different flavors. Or play with the amount of hops. It's like having a gigantic chemistry set to play with.

"I enjoy my work."

She threads her arm through mine. "You're here now. Let's have some fun."

I drag my feet. "What kind of fun?"

My friends are troublemakers. Don't get me wrong. I love them to pieces. They are supportive and don't judge me. But they are troublemakers to their bones.

"Don't worry. We won't end up in jail."

"You always claim we won't end up in jail. Just because your brother is a police officer, doesn't mean you can commit crimes without worrying about being punished," I say as she drags me toward Chloe and Nova.

"My husband's a cop," Chloe says. "A very sexy cop." She waggles her eyebrows.

Nova sighs. "My fiancé is sexy, too."

My stomach burns as jealousy hits me. I push it down the same way I always do. I'm happy my friends have found love. But love is not for me. I've learned my lesson. And I'm an excellent student. I don't need to repeat the class.

"Where are Maya and Caleb?"

Sophia points down the hallway. "In their bedroom."

It's a good thing I know the burning in my stomach isn't an actual medical condition. Otherwise, I would worry I'm getting an ulcer.

"Good for them. They're enjoying themselves. Perhaps we should vacate the premises."

Nova glances around before leaning close to whisper. "They're not getting down and dirty."

My brow wrinkles. "What are they doing?"

"Caleb had another 'incident'."

I frown. Caleb has panic attacks. I assume they're a result of post-traumatic stress disorder from his time in the military. He recently discovered he cannot resume his active military duty status with the Army. The news has triggered him.

"Maya's tending to him?"

Nova nods. "She's good for him."

"Duh." Chloe rolls her eyes. "Those two have been in love since high school."

"I'm glad they finally got over their shit," Sophia says.

Their shit was not easy to get over with. Maya's father basically chased Caleb away with a pack of lies. Needless to say, Maya's father is a piece of shit.

We've tried and tried to convince Maya to cut off contact with her parents but she longed for their love. Until Caleb came back to town and showed her what real love is. I know Caleb has issues and he's not perfect, but I will love him forever for showing my friend she deserves better.

"Speaking of shit to get over." Nova points to Eli.

"What is he doing here? Caleb couldn't have possibly invited him."

I watch as he prowls through the room as if he owns it. Must be nice to be a billionaire who thinks the world owes him.

When no one answers my question, I return my attention to my friends. They're all sporting blank faces. Which means they're up to no good.

I aim my attention at Nova. She's the weak link here. Sophia and Chloe will never crack. They'll spend a night in jail before they admit to any wrongdoing. Ask me how I know.

Nova begins to squirm under my attention.

"Nova," Sophia warns.

"Don't make me tell Hudson you knew you could get pregnant," Chloe adds.

Nova narrows her gaze on Chloe. "Hudson has been to every doctor's appointment with me. He knows I had an IUD and didn't realize it needed to be replaced."

I latch onto the opportunity to change the subject away from Eli. I may want to know why he's here but I want to ignore him more. "How did you not know?"

She throws her arms in the air. "I wasn't paying attention. It's not as if I was having tons of sex."

I purse my lips. "Having sex is immaterial. You're a woman. You should be aware of your contraception requirements."

"Contraception requirements?" Chloe groans. "Way to make sex sound boring."

Natalia, who's standing a few feet away, perks up at the word sex. She creeps closer.

"Sex is never boring. Is Lucas doing it wrong? Do you need a new set of handcuffs?" Sophia waggles her eyebrows.

"Gross," Natalia shouts before rushing away.

Sophia glares at me. "Why didn't you tell me Natalia was behind me?"

"She needs to learn not to eavesdrop."

Chloe snorts. "The way you did?"

I purse my lips. "I only eavesdropped on Flynn and Sophia because you told me if I didn't, you'd hack into the school's database and change all my grades to D minus."

"Joke's on you. I don't know how to hack."

"I realize this. But you are beautiful. All you have to do is snap your fingers and men will do whatever you ask of them."

Chloe wrinkles her nose. "Lucas doesn't do whatever I ask."

Nova smiles. "Which is why he's perfect for you."

"I don't know. A little sex slave, who I can order around, might be fun."

"Excuse me." Lucas snatches Chloe's wrist. "I need to speak to my wife."

"Oh, goodie. I'm in trouble." Chloe giggles as he herds her away.

A baby cries and Nova sighs. "Speaking of trouble."

Hudson arrives with baby Iliana in his arms. "I think she's hungry."

"Which is the only time you allow me to cuddle my own daughter." Hudson hands Nova the baby and they disappear down the hallway.

"We're finally alone." Sophia rubs her hands together. "What do you want to do first? Replace the potato chips with kale chips? Swap out all of Maya's pictures for pictures of mermaids? Put a toilet sign on the door to the creepy basement? Put clear plastic wrap across the door to the kitchen? Start a drinking game? What about using that app you developed to cause the lights to flicker and scare everyone? Place whoopee cushions on the chairs? Stick googly eyes on everything in the bathroom?"

"Do you have any kale chips?" She shakes her head. "What about pictures of mermaids? A toilet sign? Whoopee cushions? Googly eyes?"

"Those suggestions might not work. But the others were good ideas."

I lift my eyebrow. "Really? You're going to put plastic wrap across the door to the kitchen without anyone noticing?"

She shrugs. "We can play a drinking game. Or cause the lights to flicker."

"Didn't Flynn forbid you from playing drinking games?"

"Flynn doesn't own me."

"I'm not scaring people with flickering lights. It's nearly hurricane season."

Someone behind me claps and I whirl around to find out who it is. Damn. It's Eli. I quickly whirl back around to continue my conversation – inane though it is – with Sophia but she's disappeared.

My friends suck. They abandoned me at this party knowing I don't want to get caught alone with Eli, the douchebag.

"Paisley's ruining everyone's fun again."

I turn around to face him. I don't want to be near him but I won't hide. Other than the time I hid behind the bar at the *Bootlegger*. But that was an emergency. I didn't realize he was back on the island. I hadn't had the chance to prepare myself to see him.

I cross my arms over my chest. "Would you rather pee into a toilet wrapped in plastic wrap?"

"Sophia didn't suggest tampering with the toilets."

I narrow my eyes. "How long have you been eavesdropping on my conversation?"

"I wasn't eavesdropping. This is a party. I'm mingling. You should know better. You're an excellent eavesdropper."

My face warms. Does he know I heard him all those years ago back in high school?

"Except when the door to the boy's locker room opened up and you fell inside." He chuckles.

The warmth on my cheeks spreads down my neck. Ending up on your hands and knees in a boy's locker room filled with seventeen-year-old boys was not my finest moment.

"It was a dare."

"You do realize you don't have to actually perform the dare. You can say no."

"I'm aware."

"Of course you are." He rolls his eyes. "Paisley the Perpetual Know It All knows everything."

I spit daggers out of my eyes at him. How dare he? "We are no longer adolescents. Childhood nicknames are inappropriate."

He barks out a laugh. "Still sensitive."

"Enough!"

Everyone stops speaking and I realize I shouted. Stupid Eli. He makes me irate. Whereas I can usually keep my cool in all circumstances. Even when a chemistry experiment is exploding and the entire high school has to evacuate.

I have his attention now, though. I might as well make things absolutely clear.

"I've had enough of you teasing me and degrading me. Smuggler's Hideaway is a small island but there's still enough space for us to avoid each other. In other words." I lean close to him. "Stay away from me."

I don't give him a chance to answer before I march away, straight out the door. Maya hollers my name but I ignore her. Today is her day. I'm not going to ruin it by disemboweling Eli in her living room. Cleaning up blood is such a chore.

Chapter 37

"Sex counts as cardio. I will die on this hill." ~ Maya

MAYA

"Caleb!" I call as I enter my house. No, not my house. It's our house. Caleb has been living here for nearly a month now.

It hasn't been all smooth sailing. Caleb still wallows in guilt at times and misses his career in the Army. But we make it work. We will always make it work.

I love waking up in his arms every morning. I love telling him about my day when I get home. I love hearing about his day. And I especially love spending the nights wrapped up in each other. It's a romance lover's dream come true.

I frown when I realize Caleb hasn't responded. I dig my phone out. Maybe he's working late. Sure enough. There's a message from him.

I'm at the library doing some research. Meet me here and we can walk to Smuggler's Cove for dinner?

Sure. Be there in thirty minutes.

See you soon. Love you.

I probably have cartoon hearts in my eyes as I stash my phone in my purse. I can't help it. Caleb loves me. The man I've loved since high school has loved me all along. Squeal!

I don't need romance novels anymore. I'm living my romance story. Although, I still enjoy those sexy scenes when a vampire drinks the blood of his paramour for the first time or when the werewolves realize they're fated mates.

Okay, fine. I still need romance novels. They're especially good for providing inspiration in the bedroom. I've started to read the juicy parts to Caleb in bed. It's all the foreplay we need.

Enough with the reminiscing. I need to get changed. I made the mistake of teasing Paisley about Eli and she threw a mug of beer on me. Her patience with the situation is gone. I admit I'm having more fun than I should be ribbing her.

By the time I shower, change, do my face, and wrestle my hair into control, it's been nearly thirty minutes. Shoot the mermaid! I'm late.

I nearly run to the library. It's only five minutes away since Smuggler's Rest isn't very big, but I'm gasping for air by the time I arrive. I should probably do more cardio. Sex with Caleb is apparently not enough to get me in shape.

I round the corner and slow down as the library comes into view. I frown. The lights are off. The library should be open until nine. I check my watch. It isn't yet seven. What's going on?

I try the door and it opens. Why is it dark inside if the library isn't closed?

"Caleb!" I holler.

He steps out from behind the circulation desk. I can barely make out his features since the exit sign is the only source of light in the room. "Maya."

"Why is it dark in here? What's going on?"

"There was some sort of power surge. They're working on it."

"Is there anything I can do to help?"

"I'm glad you asked. I promised one of the guests I'd bring him a book but I can't find it in the dark."

"What are you doing promising guests to bring them books? You're supposed to be the head of security."

He chuckles. "My Maya, always ready to come to my defense."

"Sorry. It seemed odd is all."

"Wesley, the front desk manager, asked me to pick it up as a favor."

"What's the book?" I can probably find it in the dark. I spent nearly as much time in the library as Paisley did, which is saying a lot.

"It's about the Pythagorean theory," he begins before giving me the exact title.

"I got this. I'll be right back. And then we can go to dinner."

I switch on the flashlight of my phone and march toward the mathematics section. I locate the aisle I want and run my finger down the books until I find the one I'm looking for. I grab it and whirl around to return to the circulation desk but nearly bump into Caleb.

I clutch my chest. "You scared me. I didn't realize you followed me."

He chuckles and holds out his hand. "I wouldn't let you run around the library in the dark without me."

We reach the end of the aisle and Caleb tugs me toward the back exit.

"Where are we going? We can't sneak out the back with a book."

He continues to lead me away from the front. What he doesn't do is answer my question.

"I'm serious, Caleb. I may have done a lot of bad things when I was in high school, but I don't steal books."

He chuckles. "Stealing books is where you draw the line?"

"Yep."

"You couldn't draw the line on stealing the car from driver's ed?"

"I didn't steal the car. We got lost."

"You left the island and didn't return for eight hours."

"There wasn't a GPS in the car."

He barks out a laugh. "And you didn't have a phone with you?"

"Stop bringing up my past," I grumble since I have no defense. We merely 'borrowed' the car from driver's ed but he obviously doesn't believe me.

"We're not stealing the book." He rounds the corner and I notice our favorite study room has light coming from it.

"What's going on?"

He's obviously up to something. I should have realized as much when he asked me to find a book on the Pythagorean theory. But I forget to be logical when Caleb's around. He scrambles my senses. In the best way.

He leads me to the room and I gasp. He's turned our study room into a romantic picnic spot. There's a blanket on the floor with a picnic basket on it, and a bottle of wine is chilling in an ice bucket.

"You made us a picnic."

He nods to the book. "Open it."

I notice a card sticking out of the book and pull it out. I flip it open. *Marry me.*

I lift my gaze but Caleb is no longer standing in front of me. He's on his knees at my feet holding out a jewelry box. Holy mermaids in the sea! It's finally happening.

He takes my hand. "Will you marry me, Bunny?"

"You did all this to propose to me?"

"You said you wanted a romantic proposal. I want to give you everything you ever wanted. I'm making up for those years we lost."

"We didn't lose those years." I've spent a lot of time thinking about this. "If we would have gotten together in high school, who knows if we would have stayed together. This way you had the chance to follow your dream of being a soldier without worrying if I could handle the long separations. And I got to attend the college of my choice without worrying if I was too far away from you."

"You might be right but I'm still going to make up for the years we weren't together."

"I won't stop you."

He squeezes my hand. "Starting with now. Will you marry me, Maya Jenkins? I want this to be the last time you use the Jenkins name. I want to give you my last name. I want to give you a family."

A tear leaks out of my eye and I brush it away. "You've already given me a family. You are my family."

"Then, let me give you my last name. And, once we're married, let me give you babies. We can expand our family beyond the two of us."

My heart skips a beat. He's offering me everything I've ever wanted.

"Yes."

"Yes? You'll marry me?"

"Did you expect me to say no? I practically ordered you to propose to me."

"Bunny." He slips the ring onto my finger. "I wouldn't have proposed if I didn't want to marry you."

"Do you know how many times I daydreamed about you proposing to me while sitting right there?" I point to the corner. "Except there were chairs in there. I didn't sit on the ground."

He chuckles. "My daydreams were a bit dirtier."

My panties dampen at the promise in his voice. "They were? Tell me more."

He stands and draws me close. "It's better if I show you."

"Are you going to defile me in the library, soldier?"

"I paid a lot of money for the library to close for the evening. I'm getting all the benefits I can."

"Such as a happy ending?" I waggle my eyebrows.

Caleb kneels on the blanket before pulling me down onto his lap.

I glance around at the romantic setting. "We're really doing this?"

"Having sex in the library? Hell yeah."

"No. I mean yes. We are definitely having sex in the library. But we're really getting married?"

"As soon as you figure out who your twenty bridesmaids are."

"I'll get on the list ASAP."

"But first," he mutters before his lips meld to mine. This kiss is as exciting as the first kiss we shared in this very room. Except I know where this kiss is going to lead. And I can't wait.

I can't believe this. I'm marrying the man I fell in love with while tutoring him in math in this library. But I'm doing it. I'm never letting him go. He'll need to start a war to get rid of me.

Caleb eases me onto my back and hovers over me. "I love you, Maya Emerson."

"You have to marry me before you can call me Maya Emerson."

"Don't you worry. We're getting married. I finally have you right where I've wanted you all along."

"Same, soldier. Same."

D. E. Haggerty

Love and Laughter in Every Chapter

About the author

D.E. Haggerty is an American who has spent the majority of her adult life abroad. She has lived in Istanbul, various places throughout Germany, and currently finds herself in The Hague. She has been a military policewoman, a lawyer, a B&B owner/operator and now a writer.

Printed in Great Britain
by Amazon